Bea on the Ball

Paul Sheppard

Cover Design by Luke Buxton | www.lukebuxton.com
Cover Graphics by areej_studio |

For Gráinne

Foreword

When I was a 15 year old girl - as Bea is in this story – I'd never have dreamt of playing football. For one thing, girls weren't allowed to play at my local school – it was strictly boys only – and for another, I found myself scared of all that the game appeared to represent. Although the world's most popular sport, with more than 3.5 billion fans around the globe, to me football signalled only hooliganism, aggression, drunken fans on trains and TV domination when there was usually something better on the other side! And crucially, it was for, of, and all about, only half of the world's population: men.

However, as we discover in Bea on the Ball, women's football was once more popular than men's in England. Shamefully, it was banned by the FA in 1921 who called it 'entirely unsuitable for women'. The game was then casually unbanned by the same FA in 1971, and, although for the following twenty years it wasn't given any extra resources to compensate for the total monopoly men's football had enjoyed for 50 years, the women's game has flourished. In spite of the treatment of women's footballers in not only England but in all the world's major footballing nations where similar bans were imposed, the game has professionalised, and girls now believe that they can play football and they are taken seriously.

Many years on from my own schooldays, as a middle-aged woman, it is my great privilege to sit on the board of elected directors for 100% community-owned Lewes FC. As the first pro or semi-pro club in the world to split playing budgets and resources equally between men and women, we are proud to show that we value women footballers equally to men and have finally created a level playing field for women. No surprise then, that our small East Sussex town is the setting for Bea's tale, and Lewes FC's ground - the Dripping Pan, sunken into the rolling South Downs - is the one where she and her friends are inspired by role models in FA Championship side, Lewes FC Women.

Football is a brilliant sport incorporating and instilling values in all of us that serve both on and off the pitch. It's about time that the resilience, determination, loyalty, effort, sacrifice, team-spiritedness, confidence and self-belief developed by our protagonist Bea over the course of her football journey were made accessible to all young people - girls and boys alike.

I hope this story inspires many other girls to follow in Bea's footsteps and to understand that there is now a place for them in football.

Karen Dobres,
Elected Director, Lewes Football Club, July 2021

1

Bea knelt on a chair by the living room window. 'When will he be here, Mum?'

Sandy Bagshot took a deep breath. 'When he's here, Beatriz Kathryn Bagshot.' And, repeated through a long sigh, 'When he's here.'

Bea continued to stare out, wishing for her dad's motor bike to roar up, but secretly wondering if he would ever arrive.

Only the day before, she had celebrated her fifteenth birthday with a combined party with her cousin and best friend, Jack. It made sense. Jack's birthday was on the 4th, Bea's on the 5th, so she was happy to agree to a joint party. Today, on Bea's actual birthday, her dad was taking her 'somewhere'. Bea loved a surprise.

'The surprise is going to be Dad not turning up at all,' Bea's big sister, Letitia, who liked to be called Tisha, had said when she'd been told about it. 'But then, that's no real surprise.'

'Shush, will you?' her mum had scolded. 'She'll hear you. And, Tisha, please don't look at me like it's my fault.'

'But it is your fault for getting with Dad in the first place.'

'That's all well and good, isn't it? Just remember, no Dad; no Letitia, no Beatriz.'

Sandy and Tisha were washing up and putting dishes away in the kitchen. In contrast to Bea, they looked so alike they could almost be mistaken for sisters, the same medium height, slim stature and blonde hair. The only difference, Tisha's was naturally crinkly. Bea's had the same crinkle and she shared the golden tones of hair with both her mum and sister, a feature she was pleased about as she thought it looked good against the light-coffee skin she also shared with her sister; her body shape didn't match theirs but that was a fact that never seemed to bother her.

Mum and Tisha continued to busy themselves. They'd just enjoyed the family's only proper sit-down meal of the week, a Sunday roast; chicken, fresh veg and gravy. Sandy always cooked a small chicken, once a week, when she was sure to be at home and knew she'd have the time to prepare it. The rest of the week she worked all the hours she could as a carer, looking after old folk who needed help and support in their own homes. Some of the elderly lived alone, others were couples who'd grown frail and lost the ability to care properly for themselves. Sandy loved her job, yet was frustrated by never having enough money to make ends meet, in spite of the long hours her work entailed. She'd been forced to sell the old car she had because it was just too expensive to run. Now, she went everywhere on an old scooter, in good weather or bad.

'She hasn't eaten much,' said Tisha, wrapping up the chicken Bea had left.

'She's full of excitement waiting for your dad. At least she's not doing what you did when you were her age.'

'Alright, Mum, there's no need to remind me.'

'I know, sorry.' Sandy spoke with a tinge of sadness. It had been a painful time. 'But I thought you were reaching the point of no return at one stage. Save that veg, too. It'll do for some bubble 'n' squeak tomorrow. I need to cook properly a bit more,' Sandy said. Her glance into the living room seemed to betray what she was thinking.

Tisha put an arm round her mum's shoulder. 'Hey,' she said, kissing her on the cheek. 'Y'know, it's okay and Bea isn't getting hassled at school over her weight. It's a wonder she's not losing it naturally, she never stops playing football.'

'For all we know they *are* making fun of her, although she's never said anything. Even if I had the time to cook every night, we couldn't afford –'

'Yeah, I know, good food doesn't grow on trees,' said Tisha.

A second later, they both let go, bursting out with laughter. Freed from the tension that a good laugh cures, they didn't want to stop. Their laughter continued until Bea walked into the kitchen, her face bringing them back to the reality of an absent dad.

Bea wondered how her mother and sister could act so happy when she was so miserable. 'He's still not here,' she said, before turning in disgust and walking back to her perch by the living room window. Looking around at the four magnolia walls where she was spending her actual fifteenth birthday, she felt dejected *and* rejected. Mum had done her best to break the monotony of the room with a large square mirror placed on one wall, and dotted across the rest some cheap replica prints of coastal Sussex, but today they surrounded Bea like a cage. Despite Sandy's strenuous efforts the beige living room carpet refused to let go of some stubborn stains from previous tenants, and although the blue faux-leather suite mostly covered them, today the sight oppressed Bea. Dad had refused to specify a time, like always, but Bea thought he would have arrived in the morning to spend all of her special day with her. Now, it was the middle of the afternoon. Just as her eyes began to cloud again, there was the sound of Brian Bagshot's familiar rapping at the door! She'd been so immersed in her despair she'd failed to hear his bike!

Bea shot to the door as her dad called through the letter box, 'Happy Birthday! We gonna have some fun tonight.'

In the hall he bent over to give her a big hug and then took off his silver-coloured crash helmet. His hair, a little grey beginning to betray the black, was close-cropped so never altered its shape, nevertheless, he patted his head with both hands just to make sure. After the usual clamour of his arrival had died down, Brian announced he had, 'Two pressies for my Birthday Girl.' And with that, he pulled a brand new smartphone from his leather jacket. 'It's all set up, but it's a new number, so you'll have to text everyone to let 'em know.'

'Oh my god!' Bea exclaimed. She flung her arms round her dad's neck and hugged him, but didn't see the look on her mum's face, standing in the doorway to the hall. Sandy wore a look of someone who'd lost a tenner and found a fiver.

'Look here,' said Brian, taking and switching on the phone. 'Come on, come on,' he continued, building up the tension. After what seemed like forever, he grinned.

Bea took the phone back and looked at the screen. Her jaw dropped and her face switched in a moment of disbelief. Above the code she read: **Brighton & Hove Albion v Tottenham Hotspur at the Amex Stadium, Kick Off 5pm, Sunday…**

She spun round showing her mum and sister. Then whirled back to her dad and hugged him again.

Sandy and Letitia exchanged looks.

Sandy struggled to place a pretence of pleasure on her face, hoping she was just in time to meet Bea's excited, 'Oh, mum, look!' as her daughter once more waved the screen at her.

All Sandy could think was, *how* did Brian get that top-of-the-range phone? A close second was the feeling of relief that, after all the broken promises, Bea was at last going to see a real live big match at a real live stadium.

'Come on,' said Brian, 'we have to catch the train.'

Bea ran to collect her blue puffa jacket but, when she left the hallway, the silence was heavy. Brian followed Sandy and Tisha into the living room, standing facing them with his hands in the pockets of his skinny jeans. They both noticed his refusal to look them in the eye. Although his feet were still, Brian twisted at the hips, first one way then the other, as if he'd never set foot in the room and was seeing it for the first time. Finally, he cleared his throat to break the silence, and with that the whirlwind Bea reappeared. The fuss was welcome to Brian and he called out that they wouldn't be back late as the loud pair danced out the front door; Bea straining to hurry on the five minute walk to the one-stop train ride from Lewes to Falmer, just a stone's throw from the Amex Stadium.

After they left, the house fell silent and the same thing troubled both Sandy and Tisha. Bea had not quite turned ten when her parents finally separated. Brian had been unable to find a job for a long while and was living with friends in a nearby village. 'Well, what about that?' Tisha said. 'Do you know how much Premier League football match tickets cost these days?'

'Not as expensive as that mobile phone,' replied Sandy.

'Mum, if he's involved with those people again it's going to mean trouble, and now it'll affect us because Bea has a dodgy birthday present.'

Sandy sat down on the sofa, her hands on her knees. 'Hold on, we don't know anything yet. Let me think.'

'I think you should ban Dad from this house.'

'I can't do that Tish. Please don't go on. That's enough for now. Let Bea get her birthday over, then we'll see how things are. Let's just have the radio on and later we can listen to the match.'

So, that's what they did.

Tisha sulking with her nose in a magazine, and Sandy dozing on the sofa with the radio on in the background. She rested, somewhat content with the news that Brighton were unexpectedly 3–0 in the lead by the 65th minute. She fell asleep thinking how delighted Bea must be watching the goals go in, despite her favourite men's player, Harry Kane, not scoring.

Minutes later, Sandy woke with a start. Someone was banging on the front door. She sat up as Tisha came into the room.

'Mum, it's a man. He says he's a Detective Constable, from Sussex Police.'

2

A young man who, Sandy thought, looked not much older than Tisha, stepped cautiously into the living room. Casually dressed in cords and an open-necked shirt, he took his hands from the pockets of a thick navy casual jacket. With one hand he flicked open his warrant card, but all Sandy could make out was *Sussex Police*.

'Good afternoon. I'm DC MacIntosh.'

For some reason, Tisha stifled a laugh then looked embarrassed. Sandy presumed it was nerves, but all she could think was that something awful might have happened.

'What's this about?' asked Sandy.

The Detective Constable cleared his throat. 'We're making enquiries that concern your husband Mrs, Ms…' stammered MacIntosh. 'I take it he's not in?'

After establishing that Brian no longer lived with the family, that Sandy wasn't exactly sure where he actually lived, and wasn't exactly sure when she expected to see him again, MacIntosh produced a contact card from his pocket that dropped from his fingers to the floor.

Tisha began to move towards him intending to accompany him to the door, and they almost bumped heads as both bent to reach for the card at the same time. Tisha picked it up, casually looked at one side before turning it in her fingers to check the other.

'Ah! Very sorry, Miss, Ms,' said MacIntosh starting to redden. 'If you could tell Mr Bagshot…that is, when you…if you, see him, that we're looking for him to help the police with our enquiries.' MacIntosh smiled nervously with a last quick glance at Sandy.

'I'll see you out,' said Tisha, walking into the hall with the young detective. 'What's it like being a detective?' she asked, but with a lift to her voice.

The young man sniffed, suspecting Tisha's tone to be ever so slightly mocking, he assumed the dignity expected of a detective in the police force. Or what he thought it should be. 'It has its moments, y'know,' he said awkwardly.

Tisha pouted unashamedly. 'See you again, perhaps.' She closed the front door and came back to her mother in a fit of the giggles. 'This must be the first time he's been let out on his own, his first assignment. Oh Mum, did you see his face? I think he fancied me.'

'Will you stop it?' said Sandy. 'I'm more concerned about what your father has been up to.' She walked through into the kitchen and put the kettle on. Tisha followed.

'We're out of coffee, Mum.'

'It'll be something to do with that mobile phone,' Sandy muttered to herself.

'What did you say?'

'Nothing. I'll pop over and get a jar.'

When Tisha offered to go with her to the shop opposite the train station, Sandy said she didn't want her chirping in her ear, she wanted time to think over the visit from the police.

The air was mild. The trees had that forlorn look about them, as if they'd come to the end of a spectacular party and the make-up was wearing a bit thin. Turning into the lane leading to the station, Sandy took out her mobile. She needed to discuss events with her sister.

'Hi, Aunt Sandy.'

'Jack!'

'Yeah, Mum's in the bathroom and Dad's out,' said Jack.

'All good with you? Have you recovered from yesterday?' Sandy asked her nephew.

'The party was great but I ate too much! How's Bea?'

Sandy told Jack that Bea was at the big match, and no doubt she would tell all at school tomorrow. 'Just ask your Mum to buzz me when she's free will you?'

Tisha recalled the arguments between her parents before Dad left home. Bea doesn't remember thank god, she thought to herself. She was too young to pick up on it. Either that or she just doesn't want to remember. *No*, she concluded, she *was* too young. Dad's still the great former football hero to her, cut down in his prime. Whenever Tisha thought like this she ended up confusing herself. Had Dad been bad to her? If not, why did she give him such a hard time? For a tough guy, she thought him weak. That was his problem.

With the coffee bought, Sandy's phone buzzed as she was halfway home. The screen showed, 'Sis'.

Janis reinforced what Sandy already knew. She must challenge Brian about the birthday present, but she'd have to do it out of earshot of Bea, and that might be a problem. By the time she turned into Court Road it was spitting with rain.

Tisha took the jar and went through to make them a cup each. 'Bring some biscuits, Tish,' Sandy called after her.

'No bickies,' said Tisha, handing Sandy her coffee.

'Bea?'

'She's scoffed the lot.'

'That's okay, better that than – '

'Yes, Mum, we've been there today, already.'

That evening, just after 8.30, Bea and Dad "rocked" home. That was the only way to describe how the pair of them behaved in each other's company. They were like propulsion forces, encouraging an equal and opposite reaction, one from the other whenever they were together.

'And the crowd! Tell Tisha what they were like, Dad,' said Bea.

'Seagulls, Seagulls, Seagulls…,' chanted Brian, while Bea laughed at him.

Tisha said, 'That's a stupid nickname for a football team.'

'The only thing I didn't like was that the crowd smelled of cold, sweet, fried onions.'

'How'd you know what *they* smell like?' Brian retorted. 'Is that what you get for your tea?'

'Dad!' laughed Bea.

'Yes!' said Dad, 'the roar of the hot-dogs, the smell of the crowd.'

Cue more hysterical laughing from Bea and her Dad.

'Look, I think we need to calm down,' said Sandy. 'You've got school in the morning and you'll never get to sleep.'

'And, I must be off,' said Brian looking around him.

'Your crash helmet's in the hall, Dad,' said Bea, giving him a last kiss.

Brian moved to embrace Tisha, but the look on her face persuaded him to put his fingers to his mouth and blow a kiss instead. Fortunately for Sandy, Bea had pulled out her new phone and was content to let her mum go to the door with him. In the hall, Sandy put her hand on Brian's arm. 'We have to talk.'

When Sandy came back, Bea was talking excitedly on her phone to Jack about the buzz of entering the stadium for the first time. 'I'm sitting there looking around as it filled with supporters. Even the air itself seemed to crackle with the…what's the word, Jack? – Camaraderie – the way the crowd noise swelled with one voice, and exploded every time the ball hit the back of the net. Can you imagine what it must be like to take the field in front of all those people?' Then, she paused in her excitement.

When the call ended, she said thoughtfully, 'Jack was a good footballer wasn't he, Mum?'

'Yes, he was honey, he certainly was. Now, if you don't need anything more to eat, I think you should get ready for bed.'

As she lay in bed, Bea went through all the action of the day. A day that had started with so much anticipation, had shifted into near despair, but then moved on again with Dad's arrival. It was a day she would never forget. The day she became fifteen, what she thought of as a *proper* teenager, a girl who was going to become a professional football star. An ambition, denied to girls for far too long.

She rolled onto her side and looked to the diffused light from a streetlamp, her drawn bedroom curtains making it glow softly, more like a gas lamp instead of the electric it was. She let her mind wander. When there were gas lamps, back in Edwardian times, there had been women and girls playing football. When the First World War started in 1914 and the men joined up to fight, women took on the men's traditional roles in offices, in the transport industries and in factories. To keep up morale, the government had encouraged women's football by promoting it.

She let her gaze wander from the window to her wall, where in the half-light she could make out the bright white jerseys of the ten outfield players of the Dick, Kerr Munitions factory, ladies team. She clicked on her light and looked at the women, lined up behind each other in a goalmouth.

She'd downloaded the photo from the net, printed it out and stuck it to her wall to remind her how amazing women's football had been back then. It had become so popular, that on Boxing Day of 1920, 53,000 people had crammed into Everton's Goodison Park, to watch the Dick, Kerr Ladies run out 4-0 winners over St Helen's Ladies in a charity match. Bea also knew that attendance record had stood for nearly 100 years and the reason it hadn't been broken was both simple and infuriating. Even thinking about it made Bea angry.

In 1921, the English Football Association, stuffed full of ignorant old men, declared the game too rough for females, banning games from being played on football league grounds. There was a host of unfair social, political and economic reasons behind that, mostly to do with men's advantages over women. That decision killed organised women's football, but women continued fighting the long campaign; demanding equality. It was getting better, but there was still a long way to go to approach the privileges held by today's men's game. Bea was determined to play a part in making that happen. She knew that imagination allied to strength could bring change.

Bea looked across to another white-shirted footballer on her wall. This was a giant picture of Harry Kane, the Spurs and

England hero. A brilliant forward, even if he hadn't scored today. Next to Harry was Bea's third 'white' picture. Ellen White, boasting the number 18 on her England jersey. She was a women's international striker, who'd played in three World Cups for the English national team and been the joint top scorer in the 2019 competition.

I wish I played up front, she said to herself. *I know I could do it, and be a goal scorer if I just got the chance. What do I need to do to get that chance?* It was her last thought, before she clicked off her light and sleep called full time on her day.

3

Bea and Jack walked along Southover Road after school. Jack's mum made Bea her tea on weekdays because Sandy and Tisha worked late. This arrangement suited everyone. Janis and Sandy were both reassured by the routine that saw Jack escorted home and Bea get a proper meal at the proper time. The street was ankle deep in yellow and fox-brown leaves, crisp underfoot. It seemed to Bea that she was the only one in her family to appreciate this time of the year. Her mum preferred the spring, and Tisha loved the summer but for Bea, rolling autumn into winter meant the renewal of the football season. In spite of today's grey skies, the streets of Lewes, in East Sussex still had a magic about them. The houses and buildings were so diverse and represented so many styles of ages past, from Edwardian, through to Henry the VIII and right back to the town's Norman castle and Priory.

Jack said, 'I've never asked you how long it takes you to walk home from the oblong?'

'And I've never asked you. Why *do* you call your house the oblong?'

'You obviously haven't noticed every room *is* an oblong. Our living room, the kitchen, the hall, and like all three bedrooms are that shape. It occurred to me in geometry one morning, that I live in a set of oblongs.'

'Umm…' Bea said, spotting a flaw in her cousin's logic. '*Your* bedroom's not an oblong.'

'It's not a bedroom either. It should be what posh people call the dining room. It's only a bedroom now because I can't go upstairs. Anyway, it is an oblong, it just doesn't look oblong.'

'Hmm, because all your stuff fills it out I suppose. All the stuff you need.'

'It's only since my compensation came through last year…and Petra's bed.'

'I wish we could have a dog, a special one like your Petra,' said Bea.

'She's special because of the things she does for me and the way she helps me. That way I love her more, if that's possible. She's more than a pet.'

At this end of town, one could hardly hear the rush of Lewes. Jack's *oblong* was a solid terraced house in a little street parallel to Bea's grandad's flat. No distance, yet worlds apart. Hence why her grandad, *Gramps* Royston Bagshot said that Jack lived in the, *posh street over the way.* Bea found it handy that when she visited one, it was easy to call on the other.

It had been just over three years since the car accident that killed her other grandparents; Janis and Sandy's mum and dad. Jack handed Bea his front door key and swung his wheelchair round. For some reason known only to him, Jack preferred to operate his chair up the ramp backwards through his front door. It was a practical process that worked to perfection for him to enter the *oblong.*

Petra, the yellow Labrador, rushed to greet Jack as usual, tail wagging, tongue lolling, with a big smiley face. Coming home to be greeted by Petra was very close to his favourite time of the day, even better than a smile from his special someone. Petra was Jack's "assistant" and she'd joined the family when she was two years old from the organization, *Dogs for Good*. Petra took Jack's leather school bag and ran off to place it in his bedroom. Bea loved to fondle and bury her nose in Petra's ears, secretly attracted to the musty doggy smell they gave off. But that was for later, because right now the smell of something much more savoury was in the air, and Bea's mouth watered.

'What's that lovely smell, Aunt Janis?' called Bea.

'Winter food,' Janis called back, 'I thought I'd make us a nice stew, with your favourite savoury dumplings!'

Bea joined Janis in the kitchen. 'Sounds absolutely brilliant, but it's not winter yet, is it? Not like, really,' she said, pointing to a shiny patch on the tile floor. 'Ugh, look at that.' Petra was the obvious culprit. At least Bea hoped she was.

'Wipe that with some kitchen roll for me, Bea,' said Janis, 'and wash your hands. I had to send Petra out while I was cooking. She started drooling, but I didn't notice she'd made such an awful mess.' Bea laughed, wiped the floor and washed her hands, then went to see if she could help Jack change in his bedroom.

Compared to Bea's room, Jack's was an Aladdin's cave. From the multi-coloured ceiling lights illuminating a host of assorted electronic devices, to his long wooden desk housing his computer and speakers, the room dared boredom to come out and fight. To one side of his bed, under the window, lay Petra's whopping big bed, red and black striped like the shirts of Lewes Football Club. Who needs a dining room, anyway?

Petra had already pulled Jack's shoes from his feet using her gentle mouth, and placed them together in a corner, albeit one crossed on top of the other. Bea watched as Petra tugged first at one leg of his trousers, then the other, although she was not yet adept at folding them for him! Bea did that, folding them on a hanger and attaching it to the handle of Jack's wardrobe, ready for the morning. They both laughed and praised Petra, who sat in front of Jack with her head to one side waiting for the next command. Instead, Jack asked Bea to help him get his trackie bottoms over his feet, and he could do the rest. Petra waited patiently for Jack to press a button on his chair and push a short lever for the chair to move silently forward. The dog dutifully followed, as did Bea; all heading to the kitchen table for their stew.

Janis intended to have her meal later when Jack's dad, Sean, came home. She took Petra with her, and left the cousins at the kitchen table, their rare silence broken by the clink of spoons and forks on dishes and the occasional slurp. The end of their meal was serenaded by the buzzing of their phones.

'Did you get this from Alana?' said Jack, turning his phone. Bea nodded. The next ten minutes disappeared in digital absorption interrupted only by Janis, asking if they'd had enough of this or that, followed by Petra demanding and getting their attention. After, *Thanks for a lovely tea*, and a final pat on the head for Petra, Bea started back for home.

Remembering Jack's question, she decided to time herself from door to door. It took her less than ten minutes, walking a shorter route than the one Jack always insisted upon. Instead, Bea took the more obvious route, up Potter's Lane, straight along Priory Street and Southover High Street, then over the railway bridge to Court Road. One day, she laughed to herself, rooks on Southover Road will drop a mess on Jack's head. Then he'll see sense.

Tisha had arrived back just two minutes before Bea, but their mum still wasn't home. 'I'm putting some pasta on,' called Tisha. 'D'you want some?'

Despite the lovely meal she'd just enjoyed with Jack, Bea couldn't resist, and was soon sitting down with her sister to her second, albeit much smaller, simpler tea. But before she'd finished, the landline rang. Bea jumped up to get it.

'Hi Dad, why didn't you phone me on mine?'

'Y'see honey,' said Brian, 'it's about the phone I need to speak to you.'

'It's fantastic. Did you forget to take the number?'

'No. It's…well, it's more complicated than that.'

'Complicated? What d'you mean?'

'The thing is, there's…uh, there's a fault with the phone.'

'No. It's great. There's nothing wrong with it. It's brilliant.'

'No, no…I mean…I think I have to ask you *not* to use the new phone for now… just until I get things sorted.'

'I don't get you. I've already given out my new number to everyone. I can't go back to my old one. What are you on about?'

'Bea, I've got to go. Promise me you won't use it. I can't explain properly over the phone, but *trust me*.'

'When *can* I use it?'

'Soon, honey. It's difficult to explain, and it's complicated…but soon.'

'You keep saying it's complicated.'

'Look, I'm really, really sorry. I can feel your disappointment, but I've got to go now to see a man about a job. I'll be round tomorrow. I'll explain everything properly then. Promise.'

Bea felt as if there was a very heavy weight pressing on her shoulders. In spite of it, because her dad had been so insistent, and sounded so sorry, even strange, Bea decided she'd put the phone aside until tomorrow. She was sure he would put right whatever the problem was.

'So, you'll be round tomorrow then, Dad?'

'Yep, and don't worry, I'll sort it.'

'Bye then,' Bea said softly. She put the phone down and trudged back into the kitchen, looking at the floor.

'What was that all about?' said Tisha, gathering up her empty plate. 'D'you want this? It's cold.'

Bea replied with a barely audible, 'No.'

Tisha put an arm around her shoulder. 'It was Dad wasn't it?'

Bea nodded, still looking at the floor.

'Was he on about your phone?'

Bea raised a heavy head. 'How did you know?'

Tisha stood in front of Bea, holding her at arm's length. 'Look at me. You're a big girl now. There are some things you gotta know about Dad.' The sisters' eyes met. 'He Will Always Let You Down.'

Tears streamed down Bea's face but the sadness was also stoked with anger. She shouted, 'You've always hated Dad. What is wrong with you? I fucking hate you.' With that she ran upstairs, slamming her bedroom door.

Minutes later, Sandy arrived home from a long day's work, exhausted. She dropped her bag in the hall and hung her coat over the stairs. 'Hello,' she called, 'any superstars home?' As soon as she came into the living room she sensed tension. 'Right, what's happened?'

'Who, more like it. Who's happened. Who d'you think?'

'Has your dad been round? Where's Bea?'

'In her bedroom.'

Sandy turned to make her way upstairs to Bea.

Tisha stopped her. 'Mum, I didn't handle it too well.'

'What can you tell me before I go up there?'

'It's about the phone. He phoned her. I'm not sure what he said, but she was upset. I made it worse. Sorry.'

Sandy went upstairs and knocked on Bea's door. 'Can I come in?' Without actually waiting for permission she eased the door open. Bea was lying on the bed, crying, inconsolable.

It took a long time for Bea to explain between sobs. 'Dad said I'm not to use the phone because there's a problem with it. But there isn't, Mum, it's perfect.'

'What else did he say?'

'He said he'd be round tomorrow to explain. I think he was in a hurry. He seemed in a hurry. He had to go to see someone about a job. What do you think he meant, Mum?'

'Did he call you on the landline?'

Bea confirmed that he had. 'Why, Mum, what d'you think the problem might be? The phone's working as good as anything any of my friends have got. It's brilliant.'

'I wish I could tell you, darling, but I don't know what the problem might be any more than you do. If your father said not to use it, there's a good reason. Now, Bea, look at me. I want you to give the phone to me until we speak to Dad. I know it's tough but that's the way things are sometimes, you know that.'

Bea took the phone from her pocket and, with a last giant sob, handed it to Sandy.

4

Next morning on her walk over the bridge to school, Bea thought of Dad coming that evening to explain the mystery of the phone she couldn't use. She could think of nothing else, and couldn't care less about the homework she hadn't done. She definitely couldn't go back to losing her phone now and suffer the humiliation of having to return to her old mobile. How would that make her look? 'Like a class dick,' she muttered to herself. 'There's nothing at all wrong with my phone.'

In spite of everything in her rotten life, Bea still felt sorry for Mum. Whilst Tisha could hardly remember a time when their parents didn't argue, Bea supposed they must have been good together once, or else neither she nor Tisha would be here. Tisha usually ignored Dad, or made sure she wasn't around when he called over. He used to work, Bea knew that, but things somehow started to go wrong when he lost his job. Or at least that's what she'd picked up. Tisha always said she was glad when Dad moved out. There was something Bea couldn't quite calculate about that, but she understood Dad made Mum unhappy. Yet, she still hoped things would change, still hoped Dad would come home and they could be a family again. Mum seemed to work all the time, and that probably allowed her less time to think about her own problems. But *what sort of life is that?* In her confusion, Bea began to think it might be good for her mum to find someone else, someone other than her and Tisha for company. She buried the thought.

As she approached the school side-yard, Bea saw six boys kicking a football about; the soccer early-birds, amongst whom she was an honorary girl member.

One of them called, 'Hey, *Beefy*. Here's *Beef*.'

Bea got stuck straight into the kick-about knowing this would be her only chance today. Her mum had collected a special neoprene support for Grandad's gammy knee, and Bea was to run it up to him during her lunch break. Gramps Roy seemed to Bea the only constant in her life. She loved him more than anything and didn't mind missing an hour's kick around for his sake.

By the time the school bell went, Bea was sweating loads but she didn't care. She was accustomed to ignoring the dirty looks she got from the *models*, as she called them, when everyone piled in roaring with chatter. The models were two skinny lookalikes in her class who regarded Bea with contempt. They wouldn't be seen dead playing football! Although she didn't cut their sort of fashionable figure, Bea was confident she wasn't short of admirers. Just before she took her seat she overheard chief model, Claire Clarkson snipe, 'Yuk, look at her sweating!'

Bea turned. She poked her tongue out at Clarkson, along with a raised middle finger. Then, to her credit, promptly forgot about it.

The academic morning moved on quickly for once. When the bell sounded, Bea set off at pace. Eight minutes later she knocked Gramps' door before letting herself in with the key he'd given her.

'Hi Gramps.'

'Hey, what about you my darling?' he called, hobbling to meet her in his slippers.

'Oh, you're limping badly.'

'It's only 'cos I've been sitting. I'm fit as a fiddle,' the old man said, laughing.

'Well, you'll be a lot fitter when you put this on.' Bea pulled out the packet with the knee support. 'I can give you a hand with it if you like.'

'No, that's okay, lovely, I'll see to it later. I've got sandwiches for us. They're in the kitchen. Put the kettle on.'

'Don't you need to change that old sweatshirt, Gramps? You always seem to be wearing it.'

'It's not like you think. You'll note it's not dirty. I ordered one, and three arrived, one after the other, all the same size and colour.'

From the kitchen, Bea laughed out loud, 'Crazy. I hope you weren't charged three times.'

'No. It's part of the modern-day madness,' called Gramps.

Bea came back carrying a stack of cheese and pickle sandwiches, two mugs of tea, and a packet of chocolate biscuits tucked under her arm. 'I see you have nice new cords on, anyway. I haven't seen those before.'

Gramps said, 'Don't you know that when you get older you shrink? I had to get new trousers. I used to be a six-footer and now I'm only five-ten!'

'Gramps.'

'It's a fact. Although I'm nearly the same as I always was around my waist, so that's less for the old knees to struggle with.'

'You're not old, anyway.'

Bea was proud of her Grandfather. He still had all his hair, snow white contrasting with his dark skin that bore deep laughter lines, and fewer wrinkles than many men nearing seventy. As the pair sat munching the sandwiches the conversation soon turned to football, their favourite subject.

It wasn't long before she was asking about the players he had admired. She was always keen to hear his stories.

'I've told you before how difficult it was for black players to make it in the professional game in my day.'

Bea nodded. One more injustice that annoyed her.

Gramps pressed on, 'There were a few that played league football, but they got given terrible abuse. England didn't pick black players until Viv Anderson got his cap, in 1978. He was a pioneer. Front page news. I know 1978 seems a long way away to you, but it's not ancient history, you know.'

'Even if it does seem like ages ago to me Gramps, it's only in *my* lifetime that girls playing football has really taken off again. That's why I love what Lewes did in 2017,' she said, reaching for another biscuit.

'Yes indeed,' said Gramps.

The pair smiled, reflecting on a favourite topic of conversation for Bea. She'd bounced into her Gramps' kitchen a year or so before, full of the news that Lewes FC, *her* local team, were to be the first professional or semi-professional football club anywhere in the world to fund its women's team the same as its men's.

'Ah yes. *Equality FC*,' the old man said and stretched out his bad leg. 'You believe that's the start, don't you my girl?'

'I do, Gramps. We're on the way to a level playing field, and I'm going to play for Lewes one day.'

'Well, you're a good player, certainly from when I used to watch you. You've got something in you. And, you could get better if...' Gramps stopped and sipped his tea. 'Well anything's possible if you work hard...anything's possible.'

'If what?' asked Bea. 'Out with it, Gramps.'

'You're playing for your school, and you're playing with the *Femstars* on Sundays, but...' he hesitated again, before saying, 'I think you've got to get a proper regime going, and that includes your diet. You're always complaining how puffed out you get running.'

'Gramps, is that, like, a nice way of saying I'm fat? It's a good thing I'm happy in my skin and not offended!'

'You're not fat, my darling. You're speedy, but you've told me yourself how you hate running! It's stamina you need, proper fitness I should say. It's hard work y'know, and hard work doesn't come easy.'

She sat back and looked seriously at him, nodding her head in as wise a manner as she thought she could muster and then said in a cheeky tone, 'Hard work doesn't come easy. Thanks for that Gramps, that's one of your most profound pieces of advice. I'll cherish that.'

He smirked at her. 'All I'm saying—'

'Yep, I know, I'm fat. Second thoughts, I *am* offended,' she joked.

They ate their sandwiches and slurped their tea, while Gramps reminisced about Bea's grandmother. 'She'd 'ave been so proud of you. Although, y'know, she hated football. She blamed it for ruining your father's education. As soon as he was home from school he was out kicking a ball. She used to say, that's why all footballers are stupid!'

'That's not true, Gramps. At least it's not true today. There're plenty of footballers with university degrees.'

'Uh-huh, different world though in my day, even your father's, too. Football was a game for the working class, by the working class. Today, it's a *passport*, if you're lucky enough and things fall in the right place, at the right time, in the right way for you.'

'I'm never quite sure what you mean, Gramps, when you talk like that.'

'Never mind for now, honey. Just you work hard at school, as well as football. If you don't, you'll end up on the railways for forty years like me.'

'At least they gave you your magnificent clock when you retired, Gramps,' laughed Bea, referring to the majestic old mantle clock that her Gramps kept in his bedroom, out of the way.

As usual, time passed quickly when the pair got into conversation. 'I'd best be on my way then. I wouldn't miss double maths for the world.'

'Bless you, girl, and mind you don't say anything to your mother about me mentioning diet.'

On her way back to school, Bea remembered the time when Tisha had her problems with food. Maybe she still has them, she thought. She's skinny. Come to think of it, she eats main meals, but I never see her snacking on stuff. Bea didn't imagine she could ever get dragged into such a dangerous illness, or more like a *lifestyle*, because that's what it was for Tisha. All wrapped up in her ambitions to look like the girls in her stupid magazines, girls who probably didn't look like that in real life anyway. She figured they were all photoshopped. Bea had read about it. An image of Claire Clarkson and her skinny mate popped into her head and she smiled to herself. *I'm more than a match for them. I'll never allow myself to be bullied. That's just the way it is!*

The school afternoon dragged. Bea was useless at maths and allowed her mind to dwell on her phone. She got butterflies thinking about what she'd do, what she'd say, if for some reason Tisha was right and Dad had to take the phone back.

Later, on the way home with Jack for tea, halfway through a conversation about why did anyone need to do algebra, Bea asked, 'D'you think I'm fat?'

'Hey, where did that come from?' he replied. 'That's what you call a *non sequitur.*'

'A what?'

'Never mind. Just tell me where the question came from? What's on your mind?'

'Well, do you?'

'What?'

'Think I'm fat.'

'All I can say is the thought never crossed my mind. You're just you, Bea.'

Jack couldn't help laughing, when Bea said, 'Even Getgo calls me *Beef.*'

The games teacher, Mr Marks, or Getgo as the kids called him, shortened from *marks, get set, go,* often referred to Bea as *Beefy.* 'It's just that I wonder if I lost a bit of weight if it could improve my running performance.'

'What might improve *my* running performance, I wonder?' said Jack.

Immediately she felt slightly guilty, punching him playfully on the shoulder. When they reached Jack's front door he handed Bea the key as usual. Stepping into the hallway and smelling the spaghetti bolognese her Aunt Janis was cooking, any idea of diet was forgotten. First though, Bea had to follow

Jack to his bedroom to watch the pantomime from Petra that was unmissable; first one shoe, then the other, followed by the trousers, and all for one measly treat!

As soon as she finished her plate of spaghetti, Bea thanked Aunt Janis, then set off to hear what Dad had to say about her phone. Outside, the late autumn air was thin and still. Gulls could be made out in spite of the dark, busying themselves swooping and calling. Like they were teasing each other.

She thought of her school friends, who happened to be mostly boys; the years of sharing classrooms, rules the system imposed, written and unwritten to compete with your peers. What would she do if Mum had to give her birthday phone back to Dad for some reason? What could that reason be? Would she have to go back to that stupid old-fashioned mobile she'd had to beg Mum for in the first place? How much would she be teased in school for that?

Bea refused Tisha's offer to share the lentil soup she'd made, and went to change in her bedroom, full of anticipation at what Dad would have to tell her. She dragged her books out of her bag and flipped through to that day's homework.

Her mum arrived home earlier than usual. She went up to say hi, and, Bea knew, to check that she was doing her homework. By now Bea had worked herself into a bad mood, and only mumbled back.

When she'd finished the maths, put her books away and prepared her football boots and kit ready for the following afternoon, her dad still hadn't arrived. It was getting late and Bea was becoming more and more agitated. By bedtime it was clear he wasn't coming, neither had he phoned. She went downstairs.

'Mum, he's not going to come now. I need my phone a minute.'

'No, honey, I don't want you to use the phone.'

'But, where is it?'

'I'm keeping it, until we find out what your dad has got himself into this time.'

'I'm going to be top prize dick at school.'

'Bea, if I could help I would. I am honestly as disappointed with your dad as you are. Try and understand.'

'But what is there to understand? What's he doing?' she shouted.

Tisha looked up ready to join in, but unseen by Bea, a red light in her mum's eyes warned that it wasn't worth the agro.

Bea knew that her fears of losing the phone she'd been so quick to show everyone at school, were going to become the reality. The realisation bit deep. 'It's not fair. This is unreal. I'm out of here.' She ran from the room and grabbed her coat from the stairs.

Her mum hurried after her, calling, 'Bea, no, it's too late, you're not going out.'

Bea ignored the plea. She *was* going out, and was already through the front door. 'I'm going for a walk,' she cried back. 'I have to, I have to walk.'

'Please, Bea, come inside this minute.'

But Bea was already hurrying along the street.

'I'll go after her, Mum,' Tisha said, reaching for her coat.

'No. Wait, we'll give her five minutes. If she's not back, I'll have to go after her. I'm afraid you'll say something and she'll…I know you won't mean to.'

Bea moved at a brisk pace, reflecting that no one chooses their family, or their classmates for that matter! The question was, how would she deal with this at school? She walked fast enough to get her heart pumping and her breathing deep. And in little more than five minutes, not noticing the few people on the streets, she had rounded the block and was back home. Mum hugged her tight until Bea felt her crying softly. By that time tiredness was overcoming both of them and, anyway, there was little else to say on the subject. The only thing left was to let events unfold. They went upstairs together.

In bed, Bea couldn't sleep, but was glad she'd said sorry and seen Mum smile.

5

Bea set off the next morning, so down that she didn't even respond to the side-yard footballers' calls of, '*Beef*, over here!'

Instead, she spied Jack talking to her bestie, Alana Lane, and some others. Jack was popular with girls, something Bea was glad about. She was happy for him in a way that, somehow, didn't quite fit with her personal feelings. Her emotions were mixed in a way she couldn't even explain to herself. As she joined them, the talk was of video games and the latest laughs on YouTube. Over the couple of days she'd had her phone she'd made massive use of it, texting and posting pics, but now she waited for the inevitable.

'Did you get what I sent you last night?' asked Chrissie Wakefield. 'Why didn't you get back?'

There was nothing else for it; Bea answered truthfully. 'Oh, I've got a shit situation with the phone. It's my dad, he needs it back for something.'

'What's that?' said Chrissie and Alana together.

'Look, I honestly don't know. He won't even, like, tell me what the problem is. I think I might even have to go back to my old one,' said Bea, fearing she'd already given too much away.

'Sucks to be you,' said Chrissie, showing little concern.

Alana was more sensitive and sympathetic. 'Maybe by the time you get home tonight it'll have been a misunderstanding, something to do with the contract, or some stupid thing like that.'

Alana played football alongside Bea for the school, as well as for the *Femstars* on Sundays, and turned the talk to the coming match that afternoon. They were excited by the visit of the Academy team, who they were dying to beat, although it seemed an age before the 3 o'clock kick-off. The bell sounded and cued an increase in excited babble as they piled in. The walls witnessed the usual greetings, the genuine, the perfunctory, and the sly. And that was just the teachers.

At lunch time, Bea sat with Jack and Alana, listening to Jack talking about the wheelchair basketball he'd joined recently in Brighton.

'Dad bought this special wheelchair. It's much lighter than the *throne*.' The throne was Jack's name for his usual day-to-day motorised wheelchair. 'It gets pretty competitive. I even got tossed out once.'

'That sounds quite dangerous,' said Alana.

'Nah, not if you're a tough guy like me.'

The girls smiled. The kids in their school were mostly not a bad lot. Few, if any, remarked about Jack's disability in a bad way and Jack was mature about his circumstances; a *glass half-full* kid. He'd determined to do the best with what had been done to him. It had helped that the people he'd met in the months he'd spent in hospital presented with a range of mind-blowing illness and injuries.

The surgeon who worked on Jack took a special liking to him, and he for her. She even came in especially to see him on Christmas day, telling Janis that she felt he was destined to become one of them one day. 'He has a surgeon's hands,' she'd said. After the accident, Jack developed a kind of early maturity beyond his peers. Bea admired him for it, as if he refused to take part in the same sort of petty mind-game competitions everyone else seemed required to juggle with. He appeared to work effortlessly to be top of the class. Yet, at the same time, Jack really enjoyed making people laugh, particularly the girls. And they loved him for it.

'Jack,' Alana said. 'Do you mind if I ask you something? Do you miss, like, playing football?'

'Of course I don't mind. I would mind if people steered clear of asking me questions they think might hurt or offend me.'

The look Bea saw on Jack's face, as he replied to Alana, reminded her strangely of the way Petra looked at him when she rested her head on his lap. Then she had a light bulb moment: Jack was in love! Of course, it made sense. Alana lived in Grange Road, a continuation of Southover. They didn't always leave at the same time, but she bet that soon Alana would be joining them every afternoon on their way home.

Bea's breath came in lung-bursting pants – *Hur-fur-hur-fur-hur-fur* – and her head pounded. She was sweating like a lump of cheddar under a hot sun. Her boots were too small, but at that moment she ignored the throbbing in her feet. All she could think was the goal against them was down to her.

'Keep up, *Beef*. You could have blocked that,' said her goalkeeper.

No one was sure who'd coined the nickname first, but it stuck. And an embarrassed Bea felt that it was deserved after she'd moved too far upfield. The intention was good, to support her side's attack, but a long high opposition clearance fell behind her, on the right flank that she was supposed to be covering. The running she'd already put in told, and caught her out when she tried to get back to defend the breakaway. By the time one of the opposing forwards aimed the shot, although Bea had managed to recover ground and was almost in a decent position, she was simply too puffed to make the tackle. Her running at speed in short bursts was electric, but running over distance had let her down again. She knew she was a decent player getting better, and her coaches had told her that she showed signs of becoming super-skilful on the ball. She also knew her passion and persistence kept her in touch with, albeit on the fringes of, the school's best players. But her fitness?

They lost the match 2-1 to Academy, a defeat that rankled because the rivalry between the two schools went back years, and included some of the parents. After the final whistle Bea traipsed off the *Convent Fields*, deliberately hanging back, last player as usual whenever she felt at fault, or felt she'd had a poor game.

'Alright, *Beef?*' enquired Mr Marks, handing her two corner flags. 'Here, carry these over.' Bea wiped her forehead with her shirt sleeve, and took the flags. 'You're a tryer anyway, I'll give you that, *Beef.*' Before sprinting to the head of the line to supervise, he turned. 'No, you're more than that,' he said, adding, 'hard luck with their winner.'

Getgo meant well, but his comments didn't help, they only added to her embarrassment. Bea was growing uncertain how she felt about her nick-name, but then nick-names are not usually chosen by the person on the end of them. In truth she was never much bothered by the nick-name before now. Maybe things were changing.

The studs of the players click-clacked over the concrete path. In spite of the defeat, Bea watched her team's forwards

34

receive claps on the back and commiserations from the school supporters. This made her more determined she was going to become a much better player. One day, she was going to be a professional footballer, through sheer effort allied with the natural skills she knew she had. *Yeah, in your dreams*, said the voice in her head... The logical Bea. *No*, she countered, same head, different voice. I *am* going to change!

Tisha was half-sitting half-lying on one of the armchairs, her knees drawn up with a magazine across them. 'How'd it go?' she asked, absent-mindedly flicking over a page.

'Lost, two-one.'

'Ne'mind, babes, cheer up, Academy's a good side.'

Bea could get very frustrated with her sis at times. Tisha had played football too, before she left school and her training in beauty therapy took up all her time. Now she always had her face in some make-up magazine. Although she'd never had Bea's passion, she still enjoyed discussing the game with her sometimes, but she'd never shared Bea's ideas that the women's game could compete with the men's. Putting her magazine down, Tisha said, 'And anyway, I don't suppose there were that many there to watch?'

Bea countered, 'Maybe not, but that'll change.'

'Yeah, right,' Tisha said sarcastically.

'If you knew your history, you'd know women's football *was* huge. It will be again.'

'Yeah, but you make it sound like...the whole world. The world of girl's football is a small one,' argued Tisha. 'It'll never rival the men's, that's all I'm saying.'

'You don't even know how big *Equality FC* is getting. It's a part of the growing movement for all of us now. It's known all over the world,' said Bea, 'and it started here, in this town.'

'Okay, you got me there, but –'

'Tisha,' called Mum, 'make sure Bea has a shower before her tea.'

'No probs, Mum,' Bea called back. She knew her mother was resting upstairs, just having come in from work. It was a physically hard job going round helping elderly folk, house to house. She was exhausted most days.

In the bathroom, Bea liked the way her hair just fell into shape after a shower. The natural crinkles found their own shape. She smiled as she dried herself, looking in the mirror. Mum was always saying what lovely hair she and Tisha had. Bea thrust back her head, twisting back and fore at the waist, until her hair tickled the small of her back. Tisha had recently had hers cut so that it sat just below her chin, and she sometimes straightened hers.

Back downstairs, Bea leant over and kissed her mum.

'Aww… look at you, all nice and clean.'

'Is tea ready?'

'Tisha's getting it now. I suppose you're starving again.'

After asking about the game, her mum told her Dad was now promising to come over to see her on Saturday. Bea wasn't sure if that was a good idea, or even whether he would make it at all; best not to think on it and expect him when, or if, he turned up.

'Right, pizzas are in,' said Tisha.

'Pizza again?' said Bea.

'What you saying? You love pizza.'

'I know, but like, I don't want to live on them. Pizza all the time's fattening.'

Tisha noted the look of alarm on her mum's face, knowing what she was thinking. On the evenings following a match, Bea didn't go home with Jack. Sandy was content that most days

Janis made sure the kids had a good meal after school, but Janis spent her days at home, a privilege Sandy wasn't able to share. She had a rare day off tomorrow, and was meeting Janis for coffee. She knew what she wanted to discuss with her.

6

The two sisters were sitting upstairs in the Riverside Café looking out over Cliffe High Street and the River Ouse.

There was so much Sandy wanted to say, and Janis was always there for her. The pair watched the winding river beneath them reflect the grey of the sky. Outside on the bridge, in his green jeans, blue jacket, and bright red neckerchief, a busker was doing his colourful best to invigorate an early-winter, monochrome morning. Over coffee and pancakes they talked about Sandy's relationship with Brian, his relationship with the girls, and the ever present issues in Sandy's life, work and making ends meet. But it was the newest concern, the critical one of Bea starting to worry about her weight that took over their morning.

'Oh my god, I'm stupid,' said Janis. 'I thought nothing of it at the time.'

'What?'

'The two of them were talking, and Jack laughed when Bea asked him what he thought of the teachers calling her by her nickname?'

'The teachers what..?'

'I can't say they all do, obviously, but apparently, Mr Marks, the one they call, *Getgo*, does. He calls Bea, *Beefy*. I think he usually referees the girls' soccer matches, and the kids all seem to think he's great.'

'Jan, I have to say I'm seriously unhappy about this,' said Sandy. 'You know what it could lead to. I'm going to have serious words with this Mr Marks asap.'

After shopping, and after Sandy had telephoned Mountfield School, the sisters decided to spend the rest of the day together and eat with Jack and Bea that evening. They made their way along Southover High Street, passing its 12th century church, crossing at *Anne of Cleves House* and turning down Potter's Lane, heading for Janis's house in Cleve Terrace. No matter how familiar they were with the town, they never tired of the historic buildings, reaching out with their splendour of ages past to grace the present.

Petra greeted them at the door, tail wagging wildly. Whilst Janis prepared a casserole, Sandy took the short walk to look in on Grandad at his flat, a minute's walk away.

Roy, as always, was pleased to see her. 'Sandy, c'mon in.'

'Did that support bandage help your knee?'

'Ah, well…'

'You haven't used it have you, Roy?'

'Well…you see, Sandy,' he tried to explain, 'I haven't been out yet, so…'

'Well do, and come over to us on Sunday.'

There wasn't that much to catch up on because Sandy looked in on him regularly. She soon switched the conversation to Bea, and asked if she'd said anything to him about her weight.

The old man immediately felt his heart skip. 'What can I say, Sandy? It's my fault, but Bea regularly goes on about how she hates training without a football. She doesn't like running and gets upset when she can't keep up. I know diet is delicate, 'specially with young ones. I hope I haven't said something I'll regret.'

'So do I, Roy. For goodness sake don't send her down that road.'

'Ah, she's too sensible, surely. She's different to our Tisha.'

'Are you sure about that, Roy? Has she mentioned anything about a teacher calling her *Beefy*?'

When Sandy left, the old man switched his radio on. He sat down, picked up his crossword, but couldn't concentrate. He put the paper down and allowed his mind to wander. To Roy Bagshot's thinking, everything seemed so much simpler back in the day. People knew where they stood. Rich and poor hadn't changed in spite of something the papers were calling *the wealth gap*, but the pace, the pace had changed. He remembered back, playing football in the streets of Notting Hill. Only recently he'd been telling Bea about it.

'If your mates called on you, the football pitch was your street. If you went and called on someone else, the game was in their street.'

He smiled at the memory of his youngest granddaughter, snuggling on the chair beside him as he talked. Always one for a story. Even now as a teenager.

'Tell me again about your Mum and Dad,' Bea had asked. That girl loved picking up family history from her Gramps. Even when he told the same stories over and over, she said there was always a little bit more that was new, and added to her knowledge.

'Well, it was the 22nd June 1948 when they arrived in this country. Today, it's hardly celebrated, but they call it *Windrush*

Day now. Back then, though…hard times. That's when Britain had an Empire. The Second World War had destroyed so much. Dad served in the Royal Air Force, and remembered Britain as a welcoming place, tolerant, that's what he told Mum. That was when there was a war to fight, an evil to overcome. The country advertised for people from the Empire to come and live and work, and help re-build. Mum and Dad were among the first hundreds of courageous people who responded to a call. *The Empire Windrush* was the name of the old ship that brought them to start a new life. It was a return to the mother country, what could go wrong?'

Bea had said, 'That's a lovely tale, Gramps.'

He shook himself from his reverie. What did I say to the girl? *I think you've got to get a proper regime going, and that includes your diet.* Bea was too sensible…now, let's see. He picked the paper up again. Eight letters across – obsessive desire to lose weight can lead to this.

Back at Janis's, with the casserole in the oven, the sisters took Petra to the Priory fields to let her have a run. A new sign had appeared on the edge of the field and as the dog loped about, running away from them and back again, ears flopping and tail wagging, dashing in and around Janis's legs, Sandy walked across to see what her local council had decided to erect.

In amongst a montage of images, including an artist's impression of the old Priory, a section of text told the story of the immediate area.

The Priory in Lewes was founded around 1081, and was one of the largest monastic churches in England, destroyed in 1537 on the orders of Henry the Eighth. The ruins were designated a Grade I listed building. The Priory precinct houses the fan-owned, Lewes Community Football Club, who play at their ground, the Dripping Pan. Nearby is the club's

3G, all-weather training pitch, The Rookery, called after their nickname, the Rooks.

Sandy pondered that the sign didn't say why the nickname was what it was. She reflected that perhaps tourists didn't need to know the supremacy those birds enjoyed in the town and how they had no respect for cars, pavements, or indeed, people's heads. She laughed a little and turned to see Petra gazing up at her.

When Petra was out with Jack she wore a special jacket telling her she was on duty, looking out for him. She loved going for a run when she was off duty, and could gallop at speed for her ball, which she returned to Janis's feet nonstop, barking if Janis was too slow in launching it off again! When Janis had had enough, she pointed the dog over to Sandy.

Sandy bent and retrieved the wet ball and launched it into the distance.

When both sisters had had enough, Petra was told, 'No more.' The panting dog went off with a sulk on, sniffing the grass. Finally, as the afternoon light faded, all three walked back to Cleve Terrace, ready for the arrival of Jack and Bea and the mouth-watering casserole.

From the kitchen, where Janis and Sandy were setting out the things for tea, Petra jumped up and padded out to the front door. They both looked on, amused by the way she stood, head cocked to one side, then nosing along the line between door and floor. Half a minute later the key was heard in the lock and the door pushed open. Petra danced comically, waiting to welcome Jack in. In reverse, he maneuvered his chair up the low wooden ramp, and pivoted round. Petra rested her head on his knees, tail whirling but feet steady, whilst he fondled her ears. Then she turned to Bea to be made a fuss of, but Bea flung the keys to the floor. Petra turned straight away, retrieved the keys and planted them gently in Jack's lap. Everyone laughed.

True to routine, Jack went to his room with Petra to help him change. This time Bea didn't join him, but went through to the kitchen. Sandy would have liked to hear something of her daughter's day at school, but Bea was only interested in one topic.

'Have you spoken to Dad?'

'I haven't heard from him, no.'

'Lovely casserole for tea,' said Aunt Janis, trying to change the subject.

They all sat down to eat, and Bea's mood lightened. The phone was forgotten for the time being. But when their meal was over and the small talk exhausted, Jack took out his phone and Bea stiffened. All the peer humiliation flooded back to her. Soon after, they exchanged their goodbyes.

Outside, Bea reacted again, but this time with silence as they walked briskly on a crisp evening. The clouds of the day had shifted, but the unspoken prevented mother and daughter enjoying a starry sky. The silence continued all the way home.

'What's wrong with her?' Tisha asked, when they reached home and Bea headed straight upstairs.

'That damned phone, of course, and your father.'

A rapping on the front door drew Bea to her bedroom window to look out. She could see nothing. It obviously wasn't Dad, so she took little notice of the voices in the hall, and got on with finishing her homework.

Tisha showed DC MacIntosh into the living room. Sandy came through from the kitchen, praying Bea didn't come downstairs.

'Evening Mrs…Ms, er…'

Sandy interrupted the young DC to end his embarrassment. 'Hello, how can I help you this time? I haven't seen my husband.'

'No. That's alright, we have. I won't keep you. I'm afraid I have to ask you to give me the mobile phone that I understand was given to your daughter. By Brian Bagshot, that is.'

Sandy went upstairs where she had hidden the phone in her bedroom. Bea's door was slightly ajar. Sandy could see her poring over her books and was thankful for that. She began to wish Brian was out of their lives, putting an end to the constant tension he created. She looked at the device in her hand, wishing she could afford things for her children that her hard work deserved. Sandy had long had the aspiration to become a nurse, but the cost of training…it was hopeless.

Downstairs she did as the young police officer asked. She looked at a handwritten receipt proffered to her by MacIntosh, with *Sussex Police* printed on it. She began to feel powerless, as if she was losing control. *I have to do something*, she thought. *First thing tomorrow morning, I'll call again. I'll insist he agrees to see me. There's no time to waste.*

7

The following day, after Bea had walked home with Jack, been entertained by Petra, and had her tea, she left early to go across the road to call on Gramps. Bea loved to admire the cabinet full of medals displayed proudly in his living room. These had been won over a number of years and belonged to her dad. Metal footballs on wooden shields with inscriptions below, each on a metal strip celebrating this or that win, in a league or cup competition. There were a number of silver footballers on plastic plinths with inscriptions, a range of individual medals, some with ribbon attached, others displayed in their small cases, one or two for losing, as well as those for winning. In all there were about thirty, won by her Dad from the time he was a boy, right through to the end of his career. He'd never made the Premiership. The biggest team he played for was Crystal Palace when they were in the Football League Championship. At twenty-five, just when he should have been reaching his best years, a serious knee injury cut short his footballing days.

'Weak knees must run in the family,' said Gramps, 'because that finished me as well.'

'My knees are fine, Gramps.'

When Bea started talking about her need to train by running over distance, and watching what she ate, Gramps wanted to change the subject. He felt guilty, and didn't want to go there. Instead, he turned the question to whether Bea was still enjoying her football.

'I don't just enjoy it, Gramps, I *love* it. You know that, why are you asking? The thing is, with the *Femstars*, it's always the same. The opposition we play is usually weak and only Alana and me and, like, one or two others take it seriously. The best thing about it is I get to play up front, but for the school I'm always in defence. You know I'm fast, but I need stamina to keep up.'

'Have you got a game, Sunday?' asked Gramps.

'*Femstars*, Sunday morning over the fields.'

'Well, Lewes Women are playing at home Sunday afternoon, two o'clock kick-off. Why don't you and your mate go along and ask someone about their junior teams?'

'Mmm, Mum likes us to have dinner around that time.'

'Well, I'm saying nothing. I'll only get into trouble,' said Gramps. 'Lewes can't have seen you play, or they'd have invited you along by now. They've got proper coaches at the club, people with all the latest knowledge who could advise you what you need to do.'

Bea walked to the kitchen and took an old cloth from one of the cupboards under the sink. 'See this, Gramps?' she said. 'It's called a duster.' And she began wiping the glass front of the trophy cabinet.

Gramps sat in his favourite chair, whilst Bea busied herself around him. His knee was hurting. He began to reflect. 'You shouldn't think badly on your dad, y'know.'

Bea said nothing, but moved on, dusting Gramps's books and furniture.

'He's not a bad lad, really. After his football finished, he got a bit lost.'

'He should have concentrated on his family, us.'

'It was the company he fell into when he started working in Brighton.'

'You shouldn't *fall* into company,' Bea retorted. 'Even I know you should choose your company wisely.'

'That time he lost his job he was offered a lot of money for storing some boxes, no questions asked. He thought it was too good to turn down. Afterwards he was retraining. You were only young. He was thinking of you, then...but they kept coming back. There wasn't a lot of money.'

'Gramps, he gambled the money he made from football. Tisha told me. I can remember people calling at our house with loads of boxes of stuff. Mum wasn't having it. That's why he had to leave, and they separated.'

Bea made Gramps a cup of tea. They embraced before she left for home.

On her way home Bea reflected. *What I especially love about Gramps,* she thought, *is he doesn't treat me like a child. He always treats me like a grown-up.*

Sandy entered the school late afternoon after the kids had gone home. She was shown to a classroom by one of the school secretaries. Mr Marks was frowning over his desk, chewing the end of a pen, a pile of exercise books open and intent on ruining his evening. He ran his hand through his hair and looked up as the door opened.

'Ms Bagshot,' announced the secretary, turning quickly and closing the door.

Sandy looked at the young teacher in the track suit who greeted her with a polite smile. The smile and his kindly face disarmed her. Mr Marks was nothing like she'd expected. Instead of a flash super-fit games teacher with more than a touch of arrogance in him, she was about to confront a vulnerable looking young man who still had a bit of the schoolboy about him. Sandy took the hand he offered in greeting, but struggled to recapture her anger at a man who had so casually referred to her daughter's appearance. The teacher sat with his hands on his knees, waiting for Sandy to speak, whilst she tried to stifle a smile thinking of his nickname, *Getgo*. She took a seat facing him, thoughts rushing back to yesterday evening and the mixture of feelings brought about by the police confiscating the phone. She cleared her throat and began, highlighting the obvious dangers for a young girl growing up, becoming sensitive about her weight.

'Are you aware of the innocent nickname they have for you?'

Getgo nodded and smiled.

'My daughter's nickname, *Beefy*, however, is not innocent. It's loaded.'

'Yes, I do see, of course. I'm afraid I get caught up in winning their approval.'

'You are not their friend, Mr Marks, you are their teacher.'

Getgo hesitated.

'Well?' said Sandy, holding the teacher's gaze.

He looked ruefully at her. 'I think I've been a bit silly,' he said. 'As I say, if only I'd given this more thought. I call many of the kids by their nicknames.'

Sandy had arrived on a mission but almost began to feel sorry for the man. He seemed genuinely naive, but his sincere response convinced Sandy her message had hit home. To reinforce it, she outlined a little of Tisha's history to make sure her concern for Bea was fully understood. Marks accepted without question; he had foolishly failed to consider the dangers in this individual instance. Instead of the intense argument she had prepared for, she found that she liked Mr Marks. Their conversation, instead of difficult, was easy and naturally it turned to Bea's passion.

'You know the women's game is really taking off, *has* taken off in fact,' said Marks. 'Bea has great control of a football and, with the right training, I think she might aspire to play professionally. She's not considered by the team as being amongst their best players, but that's because...uh...'

His hesitation was not missed by Sandy. He recovered and continued, '...she's not as mobile. But anyone who knows the game can recognise potential. She could be so good at such a young age. Top women professionals command good salaries now and prospects will get even better as we move forward.'

'Thank you,' Sandy said and genuinely meant it. Not just for his appreciation of Bea, but for his more considered use of words. 'Bea seems to think of nothing else. For a long time I thought it was just her father's influence, although her passion for football seems to grow regardless of anything.'

'You know the local club of course. I do some volunteer coaching there. I think she should pop along to the *Dripping Pan*. She might be able to join the Girl's Player Pathway. It's crossed my mind a few times, but I haven't pushed it. I suppose I thought she might have pursued it herself. I wonder why she hasn't?'

'Lewes Women play on Sunday afternoons don't they?' Sandy asked. Marks nodded. 'I prefer us to sit down to eat Sunday dinner together.'

'That's fair enough,' he said. 'But they do have other programs. There's a whole series of junior teams, from the *Rookie Kickers* under-8's fun sessions all the way through to the pathway I mentioned. Most of them wouldn't impact on or affect family time together.'

Sandy was concentrating but Mr Marks must have thought she wasn't interested. He stopped talking. 'Sorry, I didn't mean to press,' he said, looking like a kid caught with his hand in a sweetie jar.

'No. Not at all, go on, I'm intrigued,' she said and gave him a smile.

For the next few minutes Mark's filled her in on the developments at the club and how they were dedicated to ensuring first-class, formal safeguards were in place so that all the kids were protected within a thoroughly modern and professional environment. Sandy said she'd consider what he'd told her.

'One thing though, Mr Marks, I'd appreciate it if Bea learnt nothing of our meeting or what we've discussed.'

'Certainly. Absolutely,' he said, only too ready to agree.

Sandy could see how relieved he was. Mother and teacher said goodbye, each satisfied that good had been achieved.

As Sandy left the school, she was unaware of a pair of eyes following her. She wouldn't have known the young woman staring at her, but Claire Clarkson, emerging from detention, knew exactly who Sandy was.

8

Friday was the last day at school before half-term break. In spite of Dad, and the phone episode, Bea felt positive as she made her way over the railway bridge to school. It was another crisp morning, with the bluest of skies and a thin layer of frost on winter green. There were only two boys in the side yard. Bea joined them doing keepy-uppies, waiting until more bodies arrived to make sides.

One of the boys asked Bea, 'Did you see the match last night?'

Bea pretended to focus extra hard, juggling the ball purposefully with each foot. 'Don't you know that television is a curse?' she replied dismissively. 'Watching too much makes you go blind.'

The boy persisted, '*Beef*, it was Liverpool and United.'

The truth was the Bagshots couldn't afford a subscription to watch live football and Bea squirmed inside. 'Actually, I was listening to another game on the radio,' she said relieved, as if her response had been gifted to her by some benign spirit. 'Anyway, football to me is all about playing.'

'If you say so,' the boy said, clearly unconvinced.

Bea's embarrassment was saved by more bodies arriving and looking for a kick about. At the bell, she noticed the models huddled together with their hangers-on looking in her direction, but thought nothing of it. Bea wasn't scared of them, they were an irritant, simply a nuisance she didn't need. Hence she missed the build-up among the crew, the whispering and circling.

Once in the classroom, above the murmur of animated voices, Claire Clarkson struck. 'Somebody's mummy was here last night complaining to the teachers. I wonder what about?'

Most of the class looked at the models and followed their gaze directed straight at Bea. At first, she didn't respond, not even bothering to see why or where the statement was aimed. Suddenly, realising all eyes were on her, she felt a jolt in her chest. She thought to completely ignore them, but it was impossible. A middle finger wouldn't do this time. She knew nothing about her mum being at the school.

'Are you talking about me?' Bea asked.

'Well, we don't know anyone else whose mummy had to come to our school to tell tales.'

Her heart beat fast, panic rising as the class watched on. Despite her ignorance, the situation demanded a response. Struggling to keep a steady voice, Bea said, 'For a start, I don't know what you're talking about. And, if it's something to do with me it's, like, none of your bloody business.'

'If you've got a problem, *Beefy* Bagshot, you should talk to your friends about it. Isn't that what we're all encouraged to do?'

'I don't have a problem. It's you who has all the problems, because you don't like your stupid self.'

'Oh, I'm sorry. What happened to your brand new phone then? Funny how that suddenly appeared and disappeared.'

This was too much for Bea. All of her pent up humiliation and frustration spilled over. She leapt from her chair, rushed at Clarkson, grabbed her by the shoulders and threw her to the floor. The classroom erupted. Bea dropped, pinning the other girl down by the wrists. The shock on Clarkson's immaculately made-up face was priceless. Alana stood by Jack, both looking on, distressed. Amidst the yells, Chrissie Wakefield grabbed Bea around the neck and tipped her off Clarkson, before Bea could damage the porcelain face. Others stepped into the space, managing to separate the two girls as the form tutor entered the classroom. Cue that peculiar social vacuum, when all noise instantly disappears, but the intensity of excitement remains. Bodies crossed one another moving to their places, but Bea and Clarkson stood illuminated by temper.

Mrs Winks, administering a guillotine cut to the drama with her usual casual air, nodded at each girl in turn, 'I'd like to see you both after school please.' With a collective feeling of witnessing a missed penalty in a final, everyone tried to settle, but the day carried a sour excitement in class. The humiliation Bea felt wouldn't go away. There was learning to be had for sure, but not the academic kind. Wishing Dad had never given her the phone in the first place, unable to focus for the whole day, it was a good thing neither she nor Clarkson sought to antagonize the other. And still Bea was none the wiser about what the models had been alluding to.

Later, both girls stood in front of Mrs Winks. Tactically astute, she invited them to sit. Despite her comfortable body language the teacher applied her usual forensic examination skills, *what, why, where, when, how*? 'Now,' she said, 'who would like to start?'

Bea's darker skin went some way to concealing her burning embarrassment, but she sat erect and found the courage to go first. 'I honestly don't know how, or, like, why it started.'

'So, tell me first, *what* started?' said Mrs Winks. 'Claire?'

There was no hint of a blush on Claire Clarkson, who sat cross-legged. 'She attacked me, Miss.'

'Bea?' said Mrs Winks.

'I-I…in a way that's right,' Bea said quietly.

'If that's true it's very serious. Why do you think Bea *attacked* you, Claire?'

'You'd have to ask her that.'

'I'm asking you, first,' said Mrs Winks.

'I'm not sure.'

'Not a straightforward *I don't know*, then. You have some small hint of an idea?'

Silence.

'Can you help me, Bea?'

For Bea's part she was still confused over the root of Clarkson's statement that morning. Had her mother visited school? She fiddled with her fingers and wished she was wrapped in bed with the quilt over her head, safe in the moment. 'It's something she said about something that's personal. Something I haven't worked out yet, Miss.'

'Why did you make a personal comment to Bea, Claire? And what did it concern?'

'I didn't think it was a personal comment, Miss. It was an observation, that's all. And she took it the wrong way.'

Mrs Winks rose and came around her desk, settling herself on the edge of the desk and looking between the two girls. She let the moment stretch out before asking, 'Claire, did you sustain an injury, or any bruising?

'I don't think so.'

'Did you or didn't you, Claire? You've had all day to decide,' said Mrs Winks her exasperation with Claire's surly attitude becoming apparent.

'No.'

Bea fidgeted, wondering how long was this going to go on for. Her pride and confusion would not let her go so far as to offer an apology, but she needed to move things forward. She spoke up, 'I think I may have reacted badly to something she said, Miss.'

'Thank you, Bea,' said Mrs Winks. 'It's a good thing neither of you seem to have been physically injured, although I've no doubt another sort of injury has been sustained. What would you like to add, Claire?'

'Nothing.'

'In this school we learn, or I hope we do, through history and current affairs, of the agonies many people endure, much of it because they refuse to compromise, or to proffer or accept the hand of friendship. Are we going to get to the bottom of and resolve what happened this morning?' Silence.

Much to Mrs Winks' frustration it was clear neither girl was prepared to outline the provocation or retaliation behind their clash. Neither were they prepared to shake hands; both went into the detention book!

With Bea absent, Alana and Jack hung about at the station with a group of their classmates still discussing the events of the morning. Most concluded that Claire Clarkson was a bitch, and absolved Bea of blame. They knew how sensitive the subject of the phone was to her, but an element of mystery still remained. What had Clarkson been on about? Some needing to catch a train, the group broke up.

'Race you,' said Jack, as he put his chair into gear and started to tear along the pavement. Alana chased him and soon overtook the purring throne. 'Wait, wait,' Jack called. Alana stopped, and he caught up alongside.

Alana said, 'What do you actually make of the phone affair, anyway? And what is it with her Dad?'

Jack knew more than Alana about Brian Bagshot. 'He's actually a nice bloke, I like him,' said Jack. 'It's just…well I suppose he's a bit of a gangster.'

'A gangster!'

'Not exactly a gangster. I mean, he's not someone who would, like, do anyone any harm, you know. At least I don't think so. He's just…oh, I don't know. He's okay, really.'

'It's none of my business,' said Alana, 'but it's the way he treats Bea I don't like.'

'I'm going to be a gangster, anyway,' said Jack. 'I'll sit on my throne and bark orders out around the world. But, I'll be a Robin Hood character, like robbing the rich and fighting injustice!'

'Idiot. And when are you getting started on that career?'

'Tonight, right after I finish my homework.'

The racket from the rookery, the only ones celebrating the onset of a dirty, shadowy dusk, made the pair look up. Jack said, 'Bea keeps promising that one day a rook'll dump on me from a great height.'

'She's right. It'd be quicker if you went home along Southover High Street, anyway. Why *do* you come this way?' Jack's brain scrabbled for an answer. He'd speak his mind, but there were limits, even for intelligent fifteen year-old guys. Instead he shrugged and hoped for the moment to pass.

'This is your house, isn't it?' Jack said, as they passed a row of hedges and approached the first house on the terrace. 'Have you always lived here?'

'Yeah, ever since I remember anyway. I think I was about two when we moved.'

'So, really you're DFLs,' Jack laughed.

'Shh. Don't say that. Down from London is uncool in this town.'

'I was born here. Bea's a DFL though. They moved down to Brighton first, after her dad finished football. Then her mum and dad split, and they moved here a couple of years before my accident.'

'I know that bit. Bea told me. Right, so yeah, this is me, home sweet home.'

'I'd like you to come and meet my best friend sometime,' Jack said, smiling at the puzzled look on Alana's face. 'Petra,' he added before giving a wave and heading home.

Friday evening, Bea was in her room listening to the local *NewSounds* station, when Tisha tapped on her door. 'Hey, what's happening, sis? Can I come in?'

'Sure,' said Bea, taking off her headphones. 'Just no diet lectures, please.'

'No lectures, babes, but I do wanna say something and I need to get outta downstairs. Mum's listening to her 60s rubbish again. I don't know how she gets off on that stuff. It happened, like, twenty years before she was born.'

'Soul's not rubbish,' said Bea. 'Tamla Motown's great.'

'Yeah, but if I hear *What Becomes of the Broken Hearted* one more time…'

Tisha sat down on Bea's floor with her back against the wall under the window. 'Mum's worried.' She waited a few seconds, then, 'I'm worried.'

Bea sensed Tisha had an air of gravitas about her, rare, unfamiliar. She observed she hadn't got that dreamy magazine look on her face for once. Then it struck Bea they'd never had a proper sit-down talk before. Or maybe once, perhaps, ages ago when she'd had her first period. She wondered if this was what sisters did when they ceased to be children anymore. She was ready to listen.

Tisha asked Bea to remember back, back to the time when Tisha was ill. 'You *do* remember it.' She went on to describe how she enjoyed the sense of control dieting gave her. Here was a warning, but there was more. 'You can achieve what you want, safely. What I think you need to think about, is that it would complete your healthy lifestyle and is truly nothing to do with dieting. It's about being sensible. Cut out the chocolate and crisps or at least, like, cut down. Cut out the fizzy stuff, we don't need it. And the two teas thing, that's partly my fault. When you come in after tea at Janis's, I won't offer you any of my stuff. Okay?'

'This has nothing to do with Gramps, y'know?' said Bea. 'I suppose Mum told you we had a conversation?'

'I know. This isn't about Gramps, bless him. This is about you, your life and your football. That's what you've got to remember. That's all.'

'Did Mum go to the school?'

'What d'you mean?'

'Tisha?'

'What happened?'

'Only, like, that stupid bitch, Claire Clarkson, called me out in front of everyone. Said Mum had been in to see our teacher.'

'What does she know?'

'I don't know how *she* knew, but I had to hear about it from her in front of the whole bloody class.'

'On my god, listen. We've got the best mum in the world. When I was ill…I can't tell you how much it meant that Mum was there for me. She did everything, contacted everyone she thought could support me through it and help me understand what was happening. Her persistence meant people, like, professional people, came to me. I didn't have to go to them. I don't know how she pulled that off. She used to sit opposite me and we'd eat together, a mouthful at a time. If I stopped she stopped, if I didn't eat she wouldn't eat. I can't tell you the rest.

'Then, at the same time, she was coping with Dad, too. He was her child as well. He'd already had to leave by then. Maybe that's what kicked me off, I don't know. And Gramps will tell you how she helped our Gran as well. That's when we moved here. I love her to bits for what she did. I marvel how Mum survived. So, she went to the school to help you because she was mad at your nickname.'

Listening to Tisha, Bea reflected on the ordeal her mother had caused her by her visit to the school. Like a shovel of sand denying oxygen to a flame, Tisha's story had doused the distress Bea felt over the day's events. She could only think to say, quietly, 'One day I'll do something for her, something to repay her.'

'Yeah,' said Tisha. 'She deserves a life, as well.'

Bea got up and gave her sister a hug, and felt the firmness of the embrace she got back. Turning at the door, Tisha smiled, 'If you want to get fit, properly fit, do it sensibly, that's all. The boys in the kebab shop'll be heartbroken for a while, too, babes, but they'll get over it. Trust me.'

9

'Tonight's my last pizza,' said Bea. 'Okay, it won't be my last, but it's just going to be Saturday night pizza from now on.'

That morning Alana had called for her and the two girls were making their way up Chapel Hill, leading toward the golf course. Nearing the top of the steep hill they stopped to look down over Lewes. Bea remembered something her Gramps had told her. 'Some traveller, I can't remember their name, back in the 19th century, called Lewes a jewel nestling in a valley in the South Downs.'

'It is beautiful. 'Specially when the sun's shining,' Alana agreed, turning and continuing the walk uphill.

Bea was going to sleep over at Alana's tonight, where the two intended to eat, listen to the radio phone-ins on the day's football, and surf music until they fell asleep.

Alana started to talk about boys as they made their way across the Downs. The walk would stretch their legs, and the trek ahead was simply for the joy of being.

As Alana walked in front, Bea admired her. Black-haired and willowy, dressed all in black save for her green boots. Bea had begun to experience a range of feelings for her friend. She was uncertain about some things, but trusted her feelings would work themselves out.

'Jack really likes you, Lan. How do you feel about him?'

Alana was thoughtful. 'Jack's, like, really cool. He's intelligent. He's funny. He doesn't think farting is macho. He talks about stuff, and he makes me laugh. He's good looking…even sexy.'

'Wow, that's quite some positive report. Are you two getting serious?'

Alana stopped and looked across the distance to Mount Caburn. Hardly a mountain, it appeared at a distance rising as a smooth-sloped landmark, a mile and a bit east of the town. The girls, and every other kid in their school, had been taught its known history dated back to the iron-age and that during the Second World War defence positions facing the coast were dug into it to defend against invasion. Alana took out a bottle of water and each girl took a good slug.

'Well?' Bea prompted.

'I wondered about that…about, you know,' Alana said, raising her eyebrows but stopping herself short of finishing the sentence. She'd started to blush.

'From what I know, from listening to Mum and my Aunt Janis, there's no reason why not…I mean, like, Jack should be able to manage perfectly okay down there.'

'Bea!' Alana said, halfway through taking another swig from the water and almost choking. 'He's your cousin!'

'Well,' Bea said, drawing the sound out. 'That's what you meant, isn't it?'

Alana reddened a little more. 'I suppose so.' She put the top on the water. 'Come on, let's go.'

The girls ambled on the Downs for a couple of hours, chattering about everything and anything, only occasionally falling silent. On the way back, despite having walked for miles, both were still full of energy. Bea suddenly thought about her grandfather, recalling a time when he was much more active, kicking a ball about with her and Tisha, something he hadn't done in ages. She laughed out of the blue.

'What are you thinking about?' Alana asked.

'Something my gramps said to me. He said, one day he woke up to find one of his biggest fears realised. His body refused to do what his head told it! He said it felt like he was being penalised for something he hadn't done.'

'That's funny?'

'No. Not really. It was just the way he said it. He made a joke of it, making the best of it. The face he pulled just made me laugh. I was just remembering it.'

Alana laughed. 'That's why we gotta make the most of our lives, believe in ourselves. I watched something on TV a while ago. A girl about our age was saying that it seems like we'll be young forever, but we won't. I think about my health whenever I think about Jack.'

As they descended back into the town, the girls decided to look in to *Bags of Books*, a bookshop specifically dedicated to children's and young adult titles. The building seemed to have been rudely fashioned out of a centuries-old, every-which-way dwelling, sitting on the end of a charming row of terraced houses on an ancient street that had, long ago, been a main thoroughfare into the town. The door of the triangular shaped shop sat like a prow jutting into the junction of Chapel Hill and South Street and its blue paint colour reminded Bea of Doctor Who's TARDIS. She thought it appropriate as the insides always seemed to hold so much more than the small outside promised.

They spent a while browsing the shelfs, but amidst the teenage spy novels, romantic adventures, magical fantasy sagas and some more traditional science fiction, the girls couldn't find anything featuring girl's football. There was one title that celebrated the Lionesses, the English Women's International Team, but Bea had already borrowed it from the library the previous year.

'Shame there isn't a book about a teenage girl making it to the top in the Women's Super League,' Alana said.

The young women behind the counter overheard her. 'You're right, I'm afraid. I have a couple of boy's books about footballers and one about a goalkeeper, but no, no girls. Well, other than for little kids,' she said, leading Alana and Bea to a junior section. The books were marked for 7 to 10 year-olds.

'Mmm, probably not,' Bea said.

The young woman laughed. 'No, didn't think so. We have this,' she said and led them back through the curving shop to a book of facts and stats on the women's game worldwide. Alana bought it to share with Bea.

Outside, Alana said, 'Don't forget, we have to call at yours to collect your kit for tomorrow.'

'Yeah, and if I can't get new boots soon I won't be able to play at all. Seriously.'

'We could do a tour of the charity shops? They have boots for sale sometimes.'

'I'd have to mug a busker to afford even charity shop boots.'

'What would you prefer, phone, or new boots?'

'Like, don't even go there, Lan.'

Crossing South Street they bumped into a group of Year-9 guys from their school. One of them had joined a martial arts club a few months back and so his mates had nicknamed him *Bruce*. They stopped to talk, except for Bruce, who leapt around the girls pretending to deliver blows on Bea and Alana. As he circled them a tedious third time, Alana caught him firmly by the nose and gave it a painful twist.

'Arrrgh,' he shouted. 'What was that for?'

The girls walked off and Bea said, 'Yeah, I see what you mean about Jack.'

On a bench outside the old church at the end of the street sat a young observer, eating a burger. He stood up, briefly grinning to himself, before moving on. He was sixteen and knew the actors in the pantomime he'd just witnessed from school. *Budgie* was as tall as his tallest peer, with a wiry torso, broad shoulders and a shock of black hair. Sometimes he stood straight, but more often than not he held his shoulders bowed, almost in a kind of stoop. Depending on which he went with, it made him look like two different people.

Back at Alana's, she had the idea of cutting the backs of Bea's boots, an age-old trick from days long gone. They took what they thought was the sharpest knife they could find in the kitchen drawer, but it couldn't slice the tough leather. Then they found a serrated blade and managed to saw a centimetre long straight cut in the middle of the back of each boot. Bea, embarrassed, tried them on in Alana's bedroom. She felt the cuts expand each boot ever so slightly, promising to give her feet some relief. She also thought they looked awful, but it would have to do for now. After their match tomorrow, the girls planned to watch Lewes FC Women, at the Dripping Pan. Bea forced herself to overcome a trace of guilt as she considered going from the Pan to visit Gramps, to ask if he could afford to buy her a new pair of boots. She knew Mum couldn't, but Gramps might just be able to. It would be worth a try. The bottom line was that new boots were critical. It was that, or very soon, no football!

Looking around Alana's bedroom, Bea relaxed in a different world. Her parents had allowed Alana to paint three of her walls midnight blue. They'd insisted she had to have one wall white. To break up the gloom, they said.

'I wanted all black,' said Alana. 'This was the compromise.'

'I think it works,' said Bea. 'Why'd you want everything black anyway? A black room doesn't sound quite you, Lan. If I'm down I always look to you for a lift. You remind me of one of those fizzy tablets in water people take for their hangovers! You're not a gloom girl, quite the opposite.'

'Am I? Is that how you see me? I don't know. I like the Goth look, although the music's a bit crap. They won't let me do the make-up thing yet, but…' Alana gestured to her black jeans and tee-shirt.

'Goth doesn't work on me,' laughed Bea, 'but it looks cool on you.'

That evening the girls had fun trying out shades of deep purple lipstick, eye-liner, and other make-up Alana had secretly stashed away. Bea applied kohl to Alana's eyes and they painted each other's fingernails and toenails black, purple, and forest green, having a laugh and listening to *NewSounds*.

'Isn't all this stuff expensive?' said Bea.

'Shh, that's what grans are for,' laughed Alana. 'Haven't you noticed how much cooler they are than your actual parents?' Bea buried what she felt at not being able to afford things, but determined that she would call on Gramps tomorrow.

Sitting on the floor, Alana leaned toward Bea to remove a rogue crumb of cold pizza from her hair. Bea always felt a buzz when Alana said she loved her hair, the way it shaped on her shoulders, falling heavily down her back and its amazing contrast with her skin. The girls spread out on the floor head-to-head.

Alana said, 'I wonder when we'll do it?'

'Do what?'

'Lose one's virginity,' she said in a pretend posh accent, laughing.

'And who to, who with?' Bea said.

'I don't fancy Harry Kane,' Alana said, screwing her face up.

'Poor Harry then, doesn't know what he's missing. I fancy Ellen White.'

'Only you're not that way inclined.'

I'm not certain, Bea thought to herself. She wondered, too, if she was, would it affect their friendship in any way? They'd packed a lot in to their day, the walking, the talking, and the dreaming to themselves. Gradually, the pair felt waves of tiredness coming over them. Their chattering slowed and all of a sudden the floor was more comfortable. They didn't hear the rest of the house getting ready for bed and eventually both dozed off. Sometime in the night, Alana woke and shook Bea. With a stretch and a sigh they slipped into bed without exchanging another word.

Next morning, Alana's mum popped her head into the bedroom. Did the girls know it was already gone 8 o'clock? Kick-off was at 10.30 and there was breakfast to eat! Although they'd thought the walk yesterday had not told on them, the girls felt their leg muscles tight. They would need to get out on the pitch early, to ensure they stretched and limbered up. It would be a disaster to pull a muscle, or even worse a hamstring.

Alana looked in her mirror as she tied her hair back. 'Oh my God, look at my face!'

'We were so tired, you didn't bother to wipe all that stuff off before we crashed out.'

'I look hideous.'

'Come on, Lan, we need to hurry, busy, busy, busy.'

Neither could face more than toast for breakfast. They each slurped a mug of tea and piled into Mrs Lane's car. She drove to Tesco's, which was right next to the group of pitches where the *Femstars* played. Alana bought a fizzy drink for herself and a bottle of fizzy water for Bea. The girls took the short walk from the store alongside the river, then across the football pitches to the changing rooms. It was a grey sky morning, not as mild as yesterday and the wind was building. Cutting over to the community centre to change, Bea took in deep breathes, savouring the intoxicating scent of grass which always gave her butterflies in anticipation of a contest in the beautiful game.

'Don't you ever get that?' she asked Alana.

'I get excited, yeah, only I don't get the grass thing. You've got this...association. You can be anywhere near grass and you, like, come over all nervous. It's weird.'

'I wouldn't have it any other way. It's a rush I get. It keeps me buzzing,' Bea said as they entered the building. No sign of the opposition, yet.

Greeted by some of the other early-bird teammates, most of whom didn't take the game as seriously as Bea and Alana, they changed quickly. When Alana put a ball under her arm, Bea told her not to take it out with them. A ball would mean the vital warm-up and stretching they needed to do would be instantly forgotten. Their muscles still ached from yesterday's walk as the pair went through a routine of stretch and shake combined with short runs. They were soon bored, but Bea insisted. As much as Alana loved football Bea was starting to get on her nerves with her new-found strategies, however sensible they were in practice!

By the time kick-off arrived a few onlookers dotted the touchlines. The game got underway, but Bea was soon frustrated with players on both sides who obviously weren't trying hard enough for her. She was as frustrated with her own game, not seeing enough of the ball, not getting the service she wanted up front. Bea also wished the coach could be a bit more lively to inject some passion into the players, but the emphasis was purely on having a *fun* time. Although her boots felt marginally better, this had to be their last outing. These thoughts dominated and she began to lose her own focus until, just before half-time, she seized on a mistake by the opposition defence.

Using her speed to get beyond the centre-half, she collected a back pass played far too short and far too weakly. It had left the goalkeeper stranded. Running into the open space and cutting diagonally into the box, she glanced at the ball, then up to the onrushing keeper and beyond to the net. She heard her Gramps' voice as clear as if he was running alongside her, *when you get a clear sight on goal, aim low and hard across the goalie.* Bea drew back her right leg and connected perfectly. Wham! The ball hit the net. That was good, her frustration replaced by satisfaction as her teammates surrounded her. She didn't notice the man some distance away, sitting on a wall, watching intently.

At the final whistle, Bea's dad slipped from his perch and made his way home.

Bea and Alana were walking home after their 4-0 win, in which Bea had scored a hat-trick. It was gone midday already. The girls had to shower and refuel, to meet outside the Dripping Pan for the 2 o'clock kick-off. There was no time to lose, with Alana needing an extra five minutes to walk home after they separated. Although Sandy was not happy that Bea wouldn't be at home for Sunday dinner, she knew how important the afternoon was for her daughter.

Just in time, the girls met outside the Pan, wrapped up against the elements. The morning promised it, and stormy winds and rain had now set in for the day. They could hardly have picked worse conditions, but it was a chance to see a top side in action. Chelsea, of the Women's Super League, were the visitors to Lewes, of the Women's Championship. The match, a League Cup game, cost them nothing to attend because under-16s got in for free at Lewes. In spite of the rotten weather, more than a thousand fans had packed the Pan for the biggest game of the season. Bea and Alana were excited as they took their seats in the covered stand.

A close contest saw Chelsea, playing in their away strip of white, take the lead on twelve minutes through their Scottish International, Erin Cuthbert. A clever through ball from Kirby cut the Lewes' back four open and despite a brave effort by the Lewes' keeper, Cuthbert slid the ball home. It was a good effort, but the outstanding goal of the game was the Lewes equaliser in the eighteenth minute. The New Zealand International forward, Katie Rood, won the ball in a tackle just inside the Chelsea half. She belted down the left wing, Bea was impressed by her turn of speed, before cutting inside, shaping herself at the edge of the box and firing home a right foot screamer. Unstoppable! The Pan erupted!

A tense moment or two at the half-time interval, when the increasingly bad conditions prompted a pitch inspection, came to nothing as the home side, in their red and black, came back out and looked to cause a massive upset. But it wasn't to happen, despite Bea, Alana and the thousand other home supporters cheering on their encouragement.

On eighty minutes, after good chances on both sides, but with increasing pressure being applied by Chelsea, the visitor's Swedish International defender, Magdalena Eriksson, fired in after the Lewes' keeper parried the ball from a corner. Lewes tried their best, but that was the way the game finished. Not that Bea, Alana nor anyone else knew it at the time, but Chelsea would go on to win the League Cup that season, so it was a brave effort by Lewes. Still, it was a disappointment on the day.

Given the weather, the crowd was dispersing quickly and Bea and Alana were hustling along too, but they stopped at the players' steps to speak to a woman in a Lewes track suit. She told them they would be very welcome to join training with the club.

'In fact,' she said, 'we're hosting trials for the under-16 side at The Rookery. Look up The Rooks on-line why don't you? And, good luck. Sorry I can't stop to talk, just now. Hope to see you again, soon.'

'I don't know why we didn't join the Rooks sooner,' said Alana, as they made their way out.

'Yeah, agreed. We've outgrown the *Femstars*. If we're successful with Lewes, *Femstars* won't mind. Football's more of a laugh for them. We want to get serious.'

The girls battled the wind and rain to Alana's, where they parted. Bea headed on to call with Gramps, rehearsing how best to tell him about her boots along the way. Could he afford to buy her new ones? She hated asking, because she knew he lived off his pensions and also knew how expensive it was to rent a home in Lewes. It might be fifty or sixty pounds for decent boots, although the top pros probably paid several hundreds, or more! As Bea turned into the street and approached Gramps' flat, she saw Dad's motor bike parked off the road.

For some reason she didn't understand herself, Bea didn't let herself in with the key Gramps had given her. Instead, she knocked on the door, as she always did first anyway before she used her key. But this time, she waited, expecting her dad to open up, but when no one came she rang the bell. Still no one came. Could they be out in this weather, with Grandad's knee? Still reluctant to let herself in, Bea walked the few yards and looked in at the corner shop…empty of customers.

Suddenly, the sound of an ambulance siren split the early evening. It was obviously some distance away, but sounded closer by the second. The hint of anxiety she had been feeling, turned to a panic rising in her chest when the vehicle stopped outside Gramps'. She stood still, her legs unable to move. Then she saw her dad open the door to the two paramedics, a man and a woman. Why had no one come to the door for her? *Why didn't I use my key?*

Something like an electric shock ran through her, jolting her into action. Without another thought she ran across the road and straight through the open door. Voices were murmuring from the kitchen. Bea burst through, and screamed at the sight before her, 'Gramps!'

The old man was lying on the floor on his back, his face cut and bloodied. One of the medics, a woman on one knee, was speaking to him, whilst the other was pulling stuff from a bag. Then her dad came over and put both his arms round her, but Bea shrugged him off without looking at him. Her heart was hammering and she screamed, 'What's happened?'

As if they hadn't heard her the two medics took no notice, busily attending to her Gramps. Bea went to move closer but her dad held her back. She could feel her breath coming in short gasps as she looked away and then back to the medics. Then, as she felt the first sting of tears in her eyes, she saw in her peripheral vision, her dad's hand. In it was what looked like a child's cricket bat...and on that, was what looked like blood.

10

Brian followed her stare to the bat he held tightly in his left hand. 'No,' he shouted. 'No! Don't look like that Bea. What are you thinking?' He placed the thing on the floor. 'I picked it up. I was stupid.'

Bea recognised pain in her dad's voice, but her only interest was Gramps. The paramedic bending over him said, 'Easy now,' as Bea broke from her dad's grasp and bent down to reach for Gramps' hand. The old man was conscious, trying to talk between moans and groans. Tiny bubbles of blood formed and disappeared at one corner of his mouth. When they lifted Gramps onto the wheeled trolley a mask was placed over his nose and mouth that prevented him from speaking. Bea and Brian followed them out to the ambulance. At first the medics said she wasn't old enough to ride in the ambulance with them, but changed their minds when Bea pleaded. Brian said he would follow on his motorbike to the hospital in Brighton. They were soon off, with Bea sitting at Gramps' feet while the woman paramedic fussed over him, constantly reassuring him by telling him what she was doing and what was going to happen.

When they got to the hospital Bea stood feeling helpless as the paramedics checked Gramps in with a handover to hospital staff and a doctor was summoned over a speaker. A nurse took her arm and guided her gently to a plastic seat. She would have to wait until Gramps was assessed and then they'd call her, but it could be a long wait. Brian arrived by the time Bea had sat down. At the sight of him all her tension and grief erupted. She ran to him, hugged him hard and sobbed into his chest. Brian cried too, but before he could compose himself two uniformed police approached them.

Bea suddenly realised that the events packed into her day were beginning to overtake her. Her body felt heavy, but her head seemed to want to float away like some aggravated helium balloon. She sat down on the plastic seat again, not even hearing the conversation going on around her. *Mum, she had to tell Mum,* was all she could think.

But she needn't have worried. News had obviously travelled fast and only two minutes later, a kindly, concerned neighbour dropped her mum off at the hospital doors. Bea rose to meet her, and after she recounted a brief description of events, she retook her seat.

Her mum said, 'I just want to have a word with your dad.' Bea knew it was best to wait at a distance.

Sandy walked over to where the two uniformed police were.

'This is my wife,' Brian said.

Sandy was incensed. 'No excuses or lies this time, Brian. Just tell me straight what's happened, so I can get that girl home.'

'I'm explaining to these officers, all I know is I found Dad on the floor when I let myself in. He'd been beaten. I phoned for the paramedics and then Bea arrived at the same time as them. She saw the worst, I'm sorry.'

'What are they saying? How is he?'

'We don't know, yet.'

Distressed and upset, Sandy turned to the policemen, pointing at Brian. 'Will you please arrest this idiot and get him out of our lives?'

Brian stood with his head down, arms by his side. He wouldn't look at Sandy. One of the officers said, 'Mrs...er, Bagshot?'

'Yes. And please do something about this man,' she said, nodding contemptuously toward Brian.

'I'm sorry, we can see you're upset,' said the officer. 'We're trying to establish what's happened. You can be sure, if Mr Bagshot has something to answer for, then we'll take action. At the moment, he's helping us with our enquiries.'

Sandy reached into her bag and opened her purse. 'Do you know this person?' she said, handing a card to one of the officers.

'Yes. DC MacIntosh.'

'Well, Mr Bagshot is helping *him* with enquiries, too! Perhaps you'd let *him* know.' Sandy held out her hand, 'If you don't mind.' She took the card, put it back in her bag and turned on her heel.

Despite Bea's desire to wait, Sandy was insistent they go home. Finally, after the nurse who had greeted Bea on arrival had returned and given assurances that Gramps was still being assessed by doctors, she reluctantly gave in. Her dad would stay. The neighbour who had brought Sandy, gave them a ride back home.

Despite her anxiousness, fatigue overtook her and after a small tea, Bea collapsed on her bed. She didn't stir until morning. The first day of half-term.

As soon as she woke, Bea phoned the hospital. A ward Sister told her, 'Your grandad had a comfortable night.'

'I don't have school. It's half-term,' she blurted out to the Sister.

'Umm, yes?' the Sister responded, obviously unsure what that had to do with anything.

'Oh, I meant...I mean...can I come and see him?'

'Of course. Visiting time is in the afternoon. Two to four.'

Bea ended the call and dialled her father.

'Hey Bea. Let me call you back, save your call time on that phone.'

'No, Dad. I'm not having that. You won't call back. I want to speak to you now.'

'Okay honey. You know I had nothing to do with any of this?'

Although she had tried to dismiss it from her mind and she knew she had no actual proof, it wouldn't go away that her dad might somehow be connected to the horrific attack on Gramps. Her anxiety and anger got the better of her and she said, 'That's not true for a start. If it wasn't for you, nothing would have happened to Gramps.' Her assumption hit the mark.

'Bea, I've had a really long talk with the police. It might get me in trouble with...it might get me in trouble, but I'll make sure nothing like this ever happens to your grandad again.'

The realisation that she had been right made her spit her words down the phone. 'Dad, what have you done?'

He was silent.

She shouted, 'What have you done?'

'Honey, I spent the night at the hospital. Things are going to get better, you'll see. I'm getting a fresh start as a chef in a

Brighton hotel. I plan to make things happen for you, for all of us—'

'Dad, that's not what I meant. I'm not stupid.'

After another short silence, when Brian Bagshot spoke again there was a new tone to his voice. Bea recognised it as sadness. Crushing sadness with a hesitancy and a catch to his words, like he had tears spilling from his eyes. 'I'll see you soon…when Grandad is back home. I promise.'

Bea sat on her bed and looked up at the footballers all over her bedroom walls. Funny how they didn't seem to matter now. She felt low, depressed even, as if her world had no value. Her head down, Bea thought about all the lives going on without her, lives all around that didn't need her and she played no part in. It was a world bigger than any one small individual could imagine, and she didn't have the energy to compete.

Mum was at work. Tisha was at college. She was alone. She felt like crying, but no tears would come. Bad thoughts suddenly started seeping in from some place. She felt like giving up. She felt like… Something made her lift her head from her knees. A vision of Jack was before her, standing tall, his hands on his hips.

'Been there, done that! I'm disappointed in you. And, you should be ashamed of what you're thinking. I had your talent once. I had your ability. It was ripped away from me. It wasn't my fault. Worse than that, people died. It's okay to feel low, it's okay to feel down, it's okay to feel the world's against you. What's not okay is to give in! Now, no one can tell you the meaning of life, but you have a passion, and the means to go for it. So far as we know we only get one life, and setbacks are part of it. Have your dreams. Set your goals. Go for them.'

Bea got up and went for a shower.

When Bea walked into the ward she was overjoyed to see Gramps sitting up in bed with his arms crossed, looking around. She watched him closely as he fixed on her. Then he cracked a smile like a sugar lump on a sour tongue. Bea returned one the same.

'Not very pretty looking, am I?' he said.

'Gramps,' was all Bea could say, hugging him gently.

'Not to worry, honey. They're only keeping me in because I've taken a bump or two to the head. Maybe it'll knock some sense into me, every cloud and all that. If not tomorrow, they'll discharge me the next day.'

Bea examined Gramps' bruises with her eyes. 'D'you want to talk about it, Gramps?'

'Don't worry, it's nothing. Oh if only I was twenty years younger…but no, we won't talk about it now. Don't blame your dad. It was good he called in when he did. He left this morning.'

'Why do you say that, Gramps? That Dad's not to blame? We know if it wasn't for him none of this would've happened. Something has to be done.'

'Bea, please, not now,' he said and to end the conversation, he called across to a man in the next bed. 'This is my granddaughter. She's going to be a great footballer.'

Bea flashed an embarrassed smile at the neighbour, but she was determined to have her say. She took Gramps' hand. 'What d'you think we should do?'

'Do?'

'The people who did this to you…how many of 'em were there? There's bound to be more than one because cowards don't act alone. You must come and stay with us.'

'Bea, I told you, you're not to worry. Your dad'll sort it. Now, we won't say any more about it. Alright?'

She knew he wouldn't be swayed and she was a little happier at least. It looked and sounded like Gramps was going to be okay physically, just so long as he didn't get any more unwanted visits.

'Something else is bothering you,' said Gramps.

'I'm thinking.' Bea replied gloomily, 'I'm going to give up playing football for a while.'

'What d'you mean you're not playing football?'

'It's too expensive and Mum can't afford to help and I don't want to trouble her like and to top it all when you were lying on your kitchen floor, I'd been on my way to ask you to pay for new boots,' she said, her sentences all running together.

'Boots!' shouted the old man, making a few people look round at them. 'You'll have new boots before your next match.' Bea had her head down, but looked up at Gramps in his agitation. 'Not only that…there's something else I want you to have… to keep with you when you're playing.'

'What?' said Bea.

'You'll see soon enough girl. Soon enough.'

'Oh, Gramps, you're the only one I can always count on.'

Two days later, Gramps was discharged and soon settled back in his flat. He was on his feet, the bruising to his face fading, and Bea had new boots! Green, sleek, awesome!

'Snazzy!' was what Gramps had insisted on calling them, buying them after Bea had wowed at the colour. He laughed when he'd gone with her to the shop.

'These aren't football boots, they're more like carpet slippers,' he said, bending the supple leather. 'In my day, boots had to be worn in. Sometimes it'd take weeks of blisters before they began to fit, only then could you operate properly on the pitch.'

Bea had forgotten all about the something else he'd promised her.

On the Thursday evening, Alana and Bea went along to the Rookery 3G pitch to introduce themselves and to meet with the club's coaches for a training session.

Bea was nervous, as was Alana, but together they bolstered each other and anyway, they weren't the only new faces. Once all the introductions had been made the new girls joined the more experienced members and the coaches split them into two loose teams. Following a warm-up and exercise session, they played a quick training match.

Dusk was drawing in, the training lights were on and the weather was cold, but calm. Bea stood on the halfway line and felt the familiar tingle of nerves shooting through her. She wanted to do well. She needed to do well.

The first few minutes and all the action was on the other side of the pitch. She held her position, back-tracked and ran forward as the ebb and flow of the game played out and then, a loose ball, a ricochet off a midfielder, a wayward header off a defender and the ball spinning out just in front of her. She skipped in, challenged for and won it. Striding away, heading for goal, but looking up for a pass. No one in the middle, her new team mates weren't quick enough and Alana was just behind the play, no one moving into space. Undeterred, and thinking of the example of the Lewes' player Katie Rood, Bea cut inside, steadied herself and as Rood had thumped in a right-footed rocket, so Bea hammered a right-footed pile-driver past the advancing goalkeeper.

Her nerves fell away and her touches came easy for the remainder of the match. The new boots had been great, allowing her to concentrate on the game instead of the ache in her feet. Added to her performance was the fact that she and Alana already had a great sense of awareness for each other's game, so it was a surprise and a crushing disappointment to Bea when, at the final whistle, both of them were called rather sternly to one side by the head coach of the under-16s, Gemma Lynch.

'I thought we did okay,' Bea whispered to Alana.

'So did I.'

The girls stood side by side, their heads down.

'Why so sad?' Lynch asked.

The two girls looked up. The coach was smiling broadly. 'I have to say you played really, really well. If you're happy, we want to put the two of you into the team for our next match. It's an important Sussex Cup game.'

'If we're happy?' repeated Bea. 'We're ecstatic,' she said, looking at Alana, who was grinning so widely she could hardly speak.

'Welcome to Lewes and the Sussex County Women & Girls Football League. We'll get all your registration sorted and then you'll be set. Now off you go and get changed.'

Alana turned, but Bea hesitated. She nodded for Alana to go on.

Gemma waited. 'Yes Bea?'

'I…umm…I want to get fitter. To eat better and work on my stamina.'

'Ah. Excellent, but I wouldn't be worried, Bea,' Gemma said. 'Don't concern yourself. We'll work with you and map out a simple to follow training and diet regime. Although,' she added looking straight at Bea. 'If you are really serious, that's where the simple bits end and the hard work begins. Are you serious?'

'Yes. I am.' Bea said and smiled all the way back to the changing rooms.

Sunday, and Lewes Women were at home again. As they approached the Pan, Bea and Alana were thrilled by the sound. There was nothing like it even at the men's matches. There was an air-pumping, thumping rhythm, provided by The EarthQuake Drummers, who flooded the ground with sound that sparked the senses, and fired up the adrenalin. The girls laughed, believing the boom-boom-boom-boom-boom-boom couldn't fail to motivate the home team. That morning they'd played again, away this time at Newhaven, in what was their last match for the *Femstars* after officially joining Lewes.

The fact the girls were now a part of Lewes Football Club gave then an added sense of belonging at the ground, aspiring to one day turn out for the first team in the famous red and black stripe. At half-time and with Lewes 1-0 down, Bea convinced herself that, because she hadn't started the routines the coach had promised to map out for her, she should join Alana for the delicious burger and chips served up at the Pan. Take the sting of losing out of the air.

Bea envied Alana, who could stuff any amount of chocolate, crisps and fizzy drinks in and not appear to put on an ounce of weight. But individuals are different and she determined to make the best of the lot nature had awarded her. Through a mouthful of burger, Alana said, 'I didn't tell you. I'm going to Jack's tonight for tea. He invited me over to meet Petra.'

That announcement struck Bea like a dart in the heart and was all the more surprising for the feelings it brought. 'Oh…that's great,' she said, hoping she sounded convincing. She struggled to follow up, but was caught out in her confusion. *What am I feeling? Is this jealousy? It can't be. Can it? Oh God, Am I jealous of Jack for being with Alana? What is going on?* The cascade of thoughts compressed in a second, before she added, 'You'll love Petra she's, like, absolutely amazing.'

Bea studied Alana's face. She didn't seem to have detected Bea's confusion. The moment passed and the girls took their seats for the second half.

Her thoughts wandered and despite trying, Bea couldn't focus on the rest of the game. The forty-five minutes dragged on and on, in spite of goals that saw Lewes turn the match on its head, eventually running out 3-1 winners. Alana was buoyed and Bea did her best to mimic the emotion. She wasn't sure she'd succeeded.

Outside the ground the friends hugged, then separated, setting off in their different directions. On the way home Bea fought to make sense of her feelings. She didn't want to have to talk to Mum and Tisha, but she also knew from so many other conversations with her mum, that nothing was off limits. No topic of conversation was too difficult, nothing was too awkward and certainly nothing was ever embarrassing enough not to be spoken about. She thanked the moon and the stars for the luck of having her mum and her sister. Opening the door, she didn't hesitate and went straight in to the living room.

Sandy was on the sofa with her feet up, looking sleepy. Dishes were piled up in the kitchen. Her mum had obviously collapsed after the Sunday dinner.

'We heard the noise from here!' she said sleepily, but with a smile around her eyes.

Bea froze. The words wouldn't come.

'I take it you won?' her mum asked.

Bea murmured acknowledgement, reported the score of the game, said she didn't want the dinner saved for her yet, but perhaps later and then, despite her initial resolve said she was going for a short lie-down. She met Tisha on the landing. 'You look almost as wrecked as Mum,' her sister laughed.

'She should get herself a fit man.'

'Bea! Where did that come from. That's not like you.'

'I know. The thought is actually disgusting.'

'That's not what I meant. And, it's not disgusting.'

'Well, I think it is,' snapped Bea.

'Well, you said it.'

'I take it back.'

Tisha looked bewildered. Bea had no clue herself where the outburst had come from, so figured her sister deserved to look confused. She pushed past and disappeared into her bedroom.

'Hormonal teenager,' Tisha said under her breath.

Bea lay on her bed with her hands behind her head. She turned on her side and waited for sleep to come. In an hour, Alana would arrive at Jack's. When Jack introduced them, Petra would make a fuss of her, licking her hands, and licking her neck if Alana let her. Alana would meet Janis, and Jack's dad, Uncle Sean, if he wasn't working away. They would sit and have tea, and laugh at Petra doing things for Jack. Then they would go to Jack's room. Bea knew there was no way she was going to doze. She'd had no time to shower after the game at Newhaven, so she jumped up and got under the hot water. Beginning to feel better, she decided to write down a list of what it was that was bugging her, otherwise she would never sleep tonight. That usually worked, getting things down on paper. *But what will I write?*

11

Bea *did* write that night but, because she was unable to put her feelings into words, what she wrote had nothing to do with Alana or Jack. For now, there were no words. Instead, Bea made a list of the skills she wanted to discuss with the Lewes coaches. She had already cut back on sugary foods, eliminated fizzy drinks, and was determined to avoid fad diets. She knew that distance running would be so boring for her, yet it had to be done. She added to her list, skipping rope, sit-ups, press-ups, core exercises. The coaches already appreciated her natural ball control, so alongside building stamina and endurance, Bea wanted to build on dribbling, passing and shooting. She didn't think she would sleep well, but instead, exhausted physically and emotionally, she slept soundly and dream-free.

The next morning, she woke on hearing Mum leave for work. It was only 6.30 am, but she felt refreshed. She got up dying to pee and banged on the locked bathroom door. A stream of swear words issued from Tisha on the inside, which Bea understood meant go away and do something unmentionable! She couldn't. When you've got to go… So, after more banging and swearing, Tisha let her in to sit on the

85

loo, whilst she continued to put on her make-up, and grunt more abuse. Tisha was not a morning person.

With another whole week off school, Bea had promised to go to the Rookery. The club ran kid's community football sessions, the Rookie Kickers held on Saturday mornings and during school breaks. Sometimes one or two of the Women's first team helped out and she hoped she might get talking to them. She would have liked, as the Lewes players did, to dress in a cool track suit on the way to training, or any track suit for that matter. The one she had was too small, only fit for the charity shop. Instead she made do with changing into her kit and slipping on her warm puffa jacket. Yesterday's issue concerning Alana and Jack didn't seem to matter so much now that she was going to football. Problems always seem to retreat when you focus on your life's passion. Alana hadn't volunteered for the Rookery, so that was a good thing, for now.

At the club's 3G, the Lewes volunteers were happy to welcome Bea. She helped carry the mini-nets to set up small pitches for the little ones to kick into and have fun with footballs. The Rookie Kickers watched her doing keepie-uppies, and had great fun trying to copy her. The worst bit came at the end after the little kids had been collected, when the energy and noise left with them. It was like a void. Bea's thoughts threatened to overwhelm her again. She was rescued when a few of the seniors invited her to join them lapping the adjacent Convent Field. When her breath and body told her to stop, Bea told them to shut up! It dawned on her that she had made a start. The start. The hard work had indeed begun.

Bea met Alana and Jack separately over the course of the week. She also ran and skipped and trained mostly on her own, although Alana joined her on one of the days. The girls were strangely quieter than usual. Bea put all her effort into her running. Alana, begging her to slow down only made her train harder. Alana hadn't asked for a special training regime, but Bea was now following routines specially printed out for her. She thought she could probably have put them together herself with a little bit of research, but the fact they were issued by a real football club, a club with a history stretching back to 1885, provided inspiration and made things more real for her. In preparation for her first game for Lewes Under 16s, Saturday was a rest day. Bea headed over early to see Gramps and tell him her news.

She brought him up to speed on her final match with *Femstars* and the three goals she had scored and on the fact her new boots were fabulous. Then she launched into the world at Lewes FC. Gramps was delighted to hear the excitement in her voice, and listened happily to her describing the activities at the football club. Bea wanted to know did Gramps need anything, was he worried about anything, was he content enough? From there she called with Jack. The two of them, and Petra, met up with Alana in the Priory grounds. Alana greeted Jack with a kiss on the cheek! Bea's tummy lurched. There was that something inside she couldn't describe, that feeling she had no words for. *I need to scream*, she thought, *but scream at what? Scream at who?*

At last, as if her week couldn't go slower, the Sunday match in the Under-16s Sussex Girls Challenge Cup, against Seaford Town Girls Under-16s came around. Alana was named as a substitute, but Bea was put straight in, given the role to play up front, just off the regular Lewes centre-forward. Sandy and Tisha had come to watch Bea's first game for the club, much to Bea's nervous excitement. Sandy had mentioned her meeting with Mr Marks to Tisha, and she spied him on the opposite touchline.

She pointed him out. 'Hey Tisha, there's the games teacher. The one they call *Getgo*, there, the one with the long hair.'

'Now, that is one real man,' said Tisha.

'He helps coach at the club as one of the volunteers. He told me when we met at the school. He knew all about the club so it made sense. Come and see him up close if you think he's fit. That's what I'm here for, to find out about the set-up.'

So, the two of them made their way round to speak to *Getgo*, whilst the girls were still warming up and doing stretching exercises.

'Mr Marks,' said Sandy. 'This is my eldest daughter, Tisha.'

Marks looked genuinely pleased to see Sandy and smiled awkwardly at Tisha. 'Hello, I'm really glad you encouraged Bea to join up after all,' he said.

'The truth is I didn't. She made the decision totally on her own. I suppose we're here out of curiosity. Although Lewes has a solid reputation locally from what I've read. I hope everything will be right for her.'

'Well, I'm glad. We're all looking forward to her debut. She's impressed a few people already. As I said, she could have a future in the game. I feel guilty that I didn't propose Bea long before now.'

'Time is what it is and things happen when they're meant to,' Sandy said.

Tisha went off to get them all cups of tea and Sandy looked around the ground, taking in the details of a club that was obviously striving to be as good as it possibly could.

Finally, after a half hour of waiting and with the fetched tea being cradled to warm the hands, the game kicked off.

The cold and the wait were instantly forgotten as the match started with one of those amazing, unlikely and most definitely fortuitous things that happen in football sometimes. Lewes kicked off, the ball was passed twice from striker to midfielder and then pumped forward towards the left wing. Bea was making her run down the right. The Seaford Town defender got to the ball well in advance of everyone else, controlled it well, turned to knock it square to her keeper, but as she went to hit it, her standing foot slipped and she sliced it across the pitch. Fate had it fall to Bea who controlled it with one touch, slipped it sideways past the full-back and hit a superb curling shot that glanced off a post to nestle firmly in the back of the net. The game was twelve seconds in.

'Wow. Where did *she* come from?' said a woman next to Sandy. There was a gathering of about thirty spectators on the touchlines, and every one of them was clapping madly. Sandy could not have been more proud.

'Eh... Wow! I think you might well be right about your theory on timing,' Marks said to Sandy.

Nothing in the rest of the first half topped that opening moment and although Bea added some more good touches, she drifted in and out of the game. During the quiet spells, now that she was integrating with formal organized football, Sandy looked for reassurance from Mr Marks.

'Now Bea has joined Lewes how will she be supported? What can we expect?'

'She'll thrive, Sandy,' Marks said, one eye always on the game. 'The aim is to provide young players opportunity to learn, develop, and progress. There's every chance that with hard work she'll fulfil the potential we've all just witnessed. But with balance.'

'What if things don't work out, though, for whatever reason?'

'Well that's what I mean about balance. It's a friendly, supportive, setting and young ones make lasting friendships, don't they? If her ability didn't develop, or she lost her passion, hey, she's made friends. Win-win. And above all it's safe. Anyone who volunteers and has direct contact with the kids is only approved after being thoroughly checked-out, believe me.'

The second half was almost a repeat 'in reverse' of the first. Alana came on halfway through and Bea and her occasionally slotted a few passes together, but mostly Bea was drifting in and out until, remarkably, almost with the last attack of the game, the Seaford 'keeper flapped at a cross. The tall centre-back mishit the attempted clearance, catching it with her knee instead of her foot. The ball looped up and dropped, like it had been placed for her, onto Bea's left foot. She volleyed it cleanly. into the top left of the goal, almost hitting the exact same spot her first goal had. She didn't run around the pitch, she didn't leap up and down, she didn't slide across the ground to the corner flag. Instead, she stood stock still and raised her arms, only to be engulfed by her delighted teammates. There was just time to place the ball for the restart before the ref blew her whistle. Bea had scored both goals in the 2-0 win on her debut!

Lewes Women were away that afternoon so there was no game to attend at the *Pan*. Gramps, fortified with his neoprene-bandaged knee walked over to enjoy the later Sunday dinner with the family. As usual he was made a big fuss of, which he enjoyed in the knowledge he was welcome anytime he wanted to come over. It counted for nothing that Sandy was his daughter-in-law, and not his daughter. Brian's mum, Olivia, had loved Sandy, whom they'd known since she and Brian were kids at school. They were practically neighbours, just a few streets apart and, as they got older and things got serious, Sandy became a daily visitor in their home. Gramps' respect for her was boundless because she'd been more than just helpful to Olivia, tending her when she was ill over many long months. All of that happening after Brian had left Sandy to cope alone with two kids while he ran wild. It had saddened Gramps that his son had behaved like that, yet reinforced his love and respect for Sandy.

'You made it then, Roy,' said Sandy, smiling a welcome.

'Yes. This bandage thing is brilliant. My leg feels back in one piece. I can't thank you enough. Might even be able to get to see some of the girls' games in the future. Tell me all about it then,' he said as Bea took his coat and led him into the living room.

Tisha sat him in front of the telly. 'Thanks, Gramps,' she said, and kissed him as the old man slipped her a £20 note. The same was repeated with Bea.

As they waited to be called to the table and then during their dinner, Bea relived the game to Gramps, with even Tisha and her mum adding in how amazing the goals were. Yet Bea, her two goals apart, said she wasn't satisfied with her performance.

'Don't worry about it. It'll come now you've started your training routine,' he said, avoiding Sandy's eye. 'There is a little something else you need though, and I know what it is.'

'What, Gramps?' demanded Bea.

'You'll have to wait, but trust me. It's just a certain ingredient I have in mind that'll seal the deal on your progress.'

Sandy caught his eye and smiled. 'Not some illegal wonder drug, I hope, Roy.'

'As if...' said Gramps.

'Gramps, you can't leave me hanging like this. I need to know what you mean. It's not fair. I know you're only joking.'

'Ah, but I'm not joking,' said the old man, looking deadly serious.

'Well, you have to give me a clue.'

'A clue?' repeated Gramps, thoughtfully. 'All I'll say for now is that this is going to be a little…how can I put it? A little pact just between you and me and a friend who can't speak! And the three of us have to get together to put it into action.'

'When, Gramps?'

'Soon. Now,' he said, putting down his knife and fork, 'thank you, girls, that was absolutely delicious, best meal I've had in a long time'

Sandy said, 'Roy, I won't tell you again, come over every Sunday.'

'Well, I,' the old man hesitated. He gave a little cough, 'I know I'm welcome, girls, of course I do.' He cleared his throat, 'I have to tell you though…it's Brian. He's moving in with me tomorrow.'

12

Bea, Alana and Jack returned to school full of the joys of spring, in winter. Christmas would be the next break and Bea was determined to work hard. When she felt she was falling behind in her studies it bugged her. Gramps was constantly reminding her not to forfeit her education, as he'd done. 'I should've been tougher on your father, made him do his homework,' he liked to say. Then he would drift off with that faraway look in his eyes. 'Course, then there was your mother, in the same class at school, sweethearts. If he wasn't playing football he was chasing after your mum.'

Bea knew she'd have to get stuck into a routine comprising study, training, and match days, but there would still be a little time for having fun. The three and a group of others planned to check out a new young DJ *Blaze100* doing a gig at the youth club on Friday. The friends were talking at break, unfortunately overheard by the models.

'Oh god, are you still messing about in Lewes?' sneered Clarkson. 'We're going to Brighton. You could join us, of course, but you get *POS* and wouldn't be allowed!'

'We actually prefer parents over our shoulders, rather than ones who don't give a stuff,' Alana snapped back.

Jack rarely involved himself in sniping. For one thing he considered himself too mature for this nonsense, and it served him too, as a form of self-protection, to stay clear. This time, though, without thinking, he commented, 'Have you ever wondered why you have so few friends in school?'

'That's because all our friends have left school,' said Clarkson, with a toss of her head.

'Okay then, have you worked out why you're so unhappy?'

'Is that like your best shot? If we're unhappy, sucks to be you.'

'Come on,' said Bea. 'Let's move on.'

They shifted places, but Bea considered what Jack had said. It was true. The models didn't have friends in school. Apart, that is, from a number of the rowdier boys who flattered them by creeping around, trying to show off, and smoking. Bea supposed that, although the ones she knocked around with might not be ultra-cool, they probably had fewer hang-ups beyond the usual anxieties of growing up. And she was thankful for that.

Later that afternoon, after they'd left Alana at her house, Bea planned to call with Gramps and see what was happening with Dad. She confided in Jack. 'I think he's staying with Gramps, you know, to protect him. That's got to be the main reason.'

'I wouldn't mind meeting up with Uncle Brian again. He's a great laugh. When was it even that I last saw him?' Jack hesitated, before asking, 'Do you wish he'd come home?'

'Yes and no. Like, he made Mum really unhappy. And, Tisha, she's never got a good word to say about him. Everything he does is crap so far as she's concerned. It wouldn't work.'

'Maybe he's changed.'

'He says he's getting a job, as a chef. That's what he's good at, but Brighton is where all his trouble started.'

'Yeah, but he's not living in Brighton any more. He's in Lewes, with your grandad.'

Bea was unconvinced, but forgot about it when they turned into Jack's street. As he handed her his key they could hear Petra sniffing under the door on the inside. Life was good again.

Bea breezed into Gramps' expecting, hoping, to see Dad there. He wasn't.

'He's started his new job my darling,' Gramps informed her.

'Yes, of course. What's going to happen, Gramps?'

'Well, now. He's not just asked to live with me because of what happened. He's fed up with his life going nowhere, if you ask me. And he's ashamed.'

'Ashamed?'

'Of course, yes. There's reasons, the business of letting you down, for one…the phone…must've been tough for you, 'specially at school.'

Reasons, plural, did not escape Bea who, despite her anger, had still not worked out how to discuss the attack on Gramps with her dad. The issue of the phone was different. 'Was it stolen?'

Gramps merely looked at Bea and raised his eyebrows.

'Why does everything have to be about money, Gramps? A few people have too much, and most never have enough.'

Last summer, Bea had the great idea that she could wash her neighbours' cars for a fiver a time. It came after her friendly local newsagent had said no to her quest for a paper round, but he had let her put a free ad in his window.

Car Wash – Hello I'm Bea – Give me the tools and I'll Finish the Job! Contact…

During the long evenings and school holidays, Bea had managed to earn useful pocket money. She even had to turn some punters down, so she'd asked Alana to help her. Alana had no interest in Bea's invitation and didn't want to help. Her family didn't need the money. For a time, Bea resented her refusal but she realised it wasn't worth damaging their friendship over. It was bad enough that Bea had to have free school meals. She didn't fully understand the reasons behind something called *in work poverty*, that, in spite of people working hard, they still weren't paid enough to cover their rent, food and other bills. But car washing was a summer occupation. There was no time for washing cars during winter when it was practically dark by the time the school day ended.

Bea sat on an easy chair facing the trophy cabinet. Gramps had waited until the time was right to put his plan into action. He watched her. She took one or two of the medals and plaques out to inspect again, and perhaps dream, but when Bea closed the glass door to the cabinet, he said, 'You didn't pick up the one I wanted you to see.'

'Which one? Where? I don't see anything.'

'Then you weren't looking hard enough.'

Bea opened the door again. She scanned the shelves, until this time her eye was drawn to the bottom shelf where a dirty brown disc rested, thin with age, and totally unremarkable. Bea picked up the disc and examined it. 'There's nothing on this one. It's made out to look like a football, but there's no inscription. I haven't seen this before.'

'No. That's because it's a medal still waiting to be won.'

Bea turned the disc in her fingers. She looked puzzled. 'How did you get it? I don't understand.'

'You will, soon, but you have to work hard. Then you'll earn it.' He stood up and took Bea by the shoulders. 'Look at me. Do you believe in magic?'

Bea smiled into her grandad's brown eyes. She'd never noticed such a rapt expression on his handsome swarthy face. She smiled, 'No.'

'Neither do I.' he said. 'But when your dad was young, something I did helped him develop his game. That was his time, right now is yours.'

'What are you saying, Gramps?'

'In an old junk shop one day, that medal spoke to me. They call them flea markets today, or even antique shops if they want to attract the rich and gullible,' he laughed. 'I can't say what it was drew me to it. Sure, it was an old football medal, but with no inscription. It was a lonely medal. Waiting for something… Or perhaps someone, and I think that someone might be you.'

Bea's next proper match came midweek for the school. By this time, her training regime was in full swing. And it had begun to show. One evening Bea got Tisha to measure her height with a pencil mark against her bedroom wall.

'5 feet 3 inches or 160 cm if you prefer,' laughed Tisha. 'I'm five-six, so you're sure to catch me up.'

'Ellen White's 170cms,' said Bea. 'It says so in the book Alana bought from *Bags of Books*. That's almost 5 feet 7 inches I think.'

Everything looked good for Bea when she took the field for the school. Her running was more sustained over the course of the match, her breathing was getting easier and she was pleased with her increased stamina. She wasn't there yet and there was something else missing, something she wasn't happy with. She didn't score in the 3-3 draw and she didn't play well by her own high standards. It was time for grandad's master plan.

On school match days Bea went straight home, not to Jack's for tea. As usual, she got in before either mum or Tisha. She showered quickly, pulling her hair into shape, only taking a brief time to admire herself, as she always did from habit. Bea looked in the mirror, turning her head first one way, then the other, bunching her hair in her hand on top and still it reached her shoulders. *Should I get it cut? No*, she decided. Loads of the women footballers kept their hair long. She ran downstairs and opened a can of beans, not wanting to spend any time preparing food. She switched on the radio for some music. With the beans warming in a pan, she put two slices of bread in the toaster. When she'd finished, there was still no one home. The clocks had gone back and it was already dark outside. Gramps had asked her to bring her boots with her next time she visited him. With a smile, none the wiser about what he was on about, she picked them out of her kit-bag, and headed to see him.

The air was frosty, each breath cold as it entered her chest. As she crossed the railway bridge Bea exhaled and watched her breath condense, minuscule droplets of water forming like fleeting fog. She inhaled as deeply as she could, then emptied her lungs into the air. She smiled to herself, *I'm like a child.* By the time she reached Gramps' flat she couldn't wait to find out what he planned. She looked for Dad's motor-bike. Nowhere to be seen, but that was a good thing. He would be at work in his new job, in a Brighton hotel. She knocked then let herself in.

'Hey, Gramps!'

He was in the kitchen. Bea went through and gave the old man a hug.

'Good,' he said, 'you've brought your boots. Now tell me how you got on this afternoon.'

Bea proceeded to tell Gramps about the match, the shared six goals, and how frustrated she was that she didn't play well.

'You won't play well every game,' he assured her, 'but you've heard the saying – form is fleeting, class is permanent.'

'What's all this, Gramps? Why did you want to see my boots. Like, what *are* you going to do?'

'I want you to go and fetch our lonely medal,' he said, poring over one of the boots.

Bea went into the living room, slid the door of the trophy cabinet open, and picked up the dull metal disc in the form of an old-fashioned football. In spite of the thin worn metal, you could still make out the pattern representing the laces that all the old-fashioned heavy footballs carried, until the revolution of their design in the 1960s.

Returning, she saw Gramps had spread an old towel across the kitchen table. On it was a vicious looking Stanley knife, a long needle and thread and her boots. Gramps took the thin disc, kissed it, and slipped it into a delicate slit he'd made in the side of the right boot's soft supple leather. Bea looked on with a mixture of alarm and amusement, concerned about the health of her boot. Neither spoke during the process. Bea stood and watched Gramps as he deftly sewed two stitches, each side of the incision. *This is madness*, she thought to herself.

'Now,' said the old man, turning to Bea and handing her the boot. 'You won't lose our medal in a match, but you can easily pull it out with a pair of Tisha's tweezers. I want you to sleep with our medal under your pillow every night. And on match days, you slip it into the pocket I've made in the boot…and believe. See?'

'Gramps, that's ridiculous. What are you saying?'

99

'In life, my darling, there are many, many things we don't understand. Agreed?'

'Yes, but—'

'Belief, is like faith. It makes unexpected things happen. Be patient, continue to work hard, *Believe*.'

'Does Dad know about this?'

'No one does, only me and you. If you're going as far as you can go in football, make it all the way even, well...like all footballers, you've got to be superstitious!'

'Gramps!'

'Unless you believe,' said Gramps firmly, 'this won't work. All I'm saying is, *Believe*.'

That night, her first with the "magic medal" under her pillow, Bea slept deeply. And what dreams she had...

Harry Kane steps into the Wembley dressing room. Bea is embarrassed, and tells Harry he can't come in here. But none of her other women teammates seem to mind. In fact they don't even look up. Harry says, 'Don't mind that now. Look. You dropped this. I think you'll need it.' With a twinkle in his eye he hands her the medal. Bea is doubly embarrassed. 'How did you know?' she splutters. Harry says, 'Just believe,' and with that he turns on his heel and disappears. The next thing Bea knows, she's on the pitch with the Cup Final underway. The noise and tumult makes her rapidly beating heart feel as if it's going to leap from her chest. Alana runs with the ball and crosses from the left wing. Bea's eyes never stray from the ball's flight path. When it dips, she catches it on her magic right boot. The timing carries a bountiful blend, a caress to the foot but with a resonant thud, a combination known only to the instinctive striker on a perfect strike. The ball nestles itself around Bea's instep, remaining comfortable there for that split-second, when the striker knows her shot is seamless, when the velocity itself takes control and the ball is carried unerringly past a diving goalkeeper into a rippling net.

13

As the Christmas break approached, Alana offered Bea a ticket to the *Dizzy Lizzies* concert at the Brighton Dome. Her dad got two tickets, but it was expensive and Bea was secretly annoyed with her. Alana never seemed to recognise that Bea didn't have the money to do things Alana took for granted. Bea struggled to make an excuse, but then disliked herself for not simply coming out and telling her *I can't afford £50*. After all, why should she be ashamed at not being able to match her best friend's good fortune? Alana was lucky enough not to have to think carefully about every little thing she bought.

Bea had carried on working hard with the Lewes FC coaching staff. It looked like a new nickname might soon have to be found for her. No one was fond of calling her *Beefy* any more. Bea's playing form had become better as she improved her stamina, match by match, until she was the leading scorer both for the school, as well as *Lewes FC Girls U16s*. Yet, her performance in the last match before the break puzzled her. Something was missing, not at all right. During the match, with every miss-hit pass and skewed shot she heard Gramps' voice telling her, *form is fleeting*, but the voice in her head was no consolation. Toward the end of the game Lewes were awarded a penalty. Bea had been slightly embarrassed when she was asked to take over the penalty kicks, fearing there might be some ill-feeling from the previous penalty-taker. This was her first opportunity, but her performance had been so poor that she wasn't confident. Her heart beat wildly as she placed the ball on the spot. Looking the goalkeeper in the eye Bea retreated her practised six steps, telling herself, *I will score, I will score.* Three steps from the ball she didn't believe. The ball sailed over the bar, and there was no hiding place. The 0-0 draw left her feeling worse!

That evening, Bea was kneeling on the kitchen floor leaning over a newspaper cleaning and oiling her boots. Tisha was off college, and the sisters were together a lot. She'd persuaded Bea to join her and her friends from college to go to a music pub in Brighton on Friday. Bea had reluctantly agreed and, as she worked at the boots, she was having second thoughts when, suddenly, she thought, *my medal!* Her heart leapt in alarm. She jumped up, sped like Lewis Hamilton through the living room, past a startled Tisha, and shot upstairs to fling aside her pillows. And there, laying there, the medal.

Tisha called from the bottom of the stairs, 'Bea. What's wrong? What the hell are you doing?'

'N-Nothing,' she called back. 'I mean…I just thought I'd lost something,'

'I thought you'd freaked out. If you're not careful you'll meet yourself coming back. Come and see what I found on YouTube.'

Bea realised she had set off for her last match without slipping the medal into her boot. How could the medal's absence have had any effect on the way she'd played? It puzzled her until she became so deep in thought she wished she could share the bewilderment she felt over it. But with who? How could she tell Tisha? How could she tell anyone? It bugged her that the medal hadn't entered her head until she got home after the match to reflect on her performance. She hadn't missed it during the game. Was that the something that was not quite right? Bea had half pretended to take Gramps seriously, with his mysterious talk about faith and belief, and superstition. She began to seriously wonder, was there something credible in it after all? Certainly there was nothing rational. She couldn't even tell Alana. Anyone and everyone would think her mad. Plus, she didn't want people to judge Gramps as a stupid, superstitious old man.

Friday came and Bea made excuses for the evening. 'What am I going to wear? How am I going to get in?'

Tisha wasn't having any of it, insisting, 'All my mates are looking forward to meeting you. Plus, Sasha knows the people who run the place. You'll be fine, it's Christmas, the pub's all-ticket tonight. And, I told you, Sasha's exactly your size. When we get to hers, she's gonna sort you out.'

At the station, Tisha introduced Bea to one of her friends who lived in Lewes, and the three caught the train to Brighton, where Sasha's mother was to meet them for the short drive to the family's home. The car filled with the usual *POS* small talk, *I hope you girls are going to behave yourselves*, and so on, until they arrived at the house. Bea was knocked out by the size of it, and Sasha's bedroom. She thought it was twice as big as Alana's, with an en-suite bathroom to die for.

It was a relief for her when Bea found she liked Sasha instantly. They were all heading for *The Last Stop* pub, just behind the seafront. Sasha said it was great for cocktails and asked Bea what music she was into. Bea wondered had Tisha told them her age. Everyone else in the group was around eighteen, Tisha's age. She mentioned it to Sasha who brushed off her concerns, telling her, 'You'll be fine when we've finished with you.' Bea didn't think she looked eighteen, but marvelled at the spread of outfits Sasha started laying out on her bed for her to try on. The girls had great fun applying their make-up expertise to Bea, who gradually forgot her anxiety, trying on one dress after another. Sam, the girl who'd come on the train with them, suddenly produced a bottle from her bag; gin. The others squealed approval, Sasha went downstairs and returned with a carton of orange juice and four glasses. Entering into the swing, Bea thought there's a first time for everything and picked up a glass.

It was still early evening when they met the others, by which time Bea thought her life was just beginning. Although she'd had only a couple of glasses she was exhilarated after the gin. She could hardly stop talking, telling them all she was going to be a professional footballer. The older girls thought she was amazing and looked superb in the dress she'd chosen and the make-up she was wearing. The party breezed into the deceptively large venue, however Bea was immediately bothered. She decided she couldn't speak so freely anymore because they had to shout to hear what anyone was saying! The group pooled equal money that took all that the two sisters had between them, but to make things simple Bea decided to follow Tisha and have the same cocktail she chose. Before the drinks were ready Bea tried getting acclimatised to the blare of the sound system. One of the girls shouted, 'I don't think much of the music in here. Like Rod Stewart for fuck's sake. Now it's the Beatles.'

'I love the Beatles,' shouted Bea.

'It gets better later,' piped Sasha.

A girl came over with seven cocktails of various shapes, sizes, and colours on a chrome tray. 'Here's how ladies.'

'Great,' said Tisha, handing a concoction to Bea. 'Say hello to *Randy Rita*, white rum, tequila, sugar syrup, cranberry 'n' soda. Bea took a big drink. 'Easy,' said Tisha. 'You'll end up being sick over us!'

'I feel *brilliant*,' said Bea.

'Yeah, but take it easy,' her sister repeated. Everyone laughed.

After a few repeat cocktails of more outlandish shapes, sizes, and colours, Bea continued to feel *brilliant*, and got up without a second thought when a man asked her to dance. The girls didn't want to lose their table, so took it in turns to go to the toilets, go for a dance, or just go for a walk about.

Later as Tisha and Bea were on the floor, just about to go back to their table, a man tapped Tisha on the shoulder. 'Remember me?'

Tisha turned with a broad smile, 'I didn't know policemen came to places like this.'

'Shh,' said MacIntosh, putting a finger to his lips. 'Not that anyone would hear you,' he said, leaning in close to Tisha's ear.

Smiling up at the confident off-duty detective constable, Tisha registered the change in him.

'Good to see you again. Can I get you a drink?'

'You can, if you get my sister one as well.'

'No problem. Is that you?' he shouted to Bea. 'Two cocktails? Come over with me.' So over they went to the bar. MacIntosh was unrecognisable from the bumbling young man who'd introduced himself weeks ago. Bea wanted to know who he was. Tisha said she would tell her later. When they got the drinks, Tisha went into a huddle with MacIntosh, holding a conversation of sorts, so Bea took herself back to their gang at the table. She continued to feel *brilliant*. She kept looking over at Tisha deep in conversation with the young man. Bea relaxed back and enjoyed the Indie sounds that had overtaken the oldies.

They'd arranged to stay the night with Sasha after much persuading between Tisha and Sandy. Tisha came back carrying another cocktail for Bea. 'Are you okay?' she asked. Bea said she was fine, but she was amused by the look in her sister's eyes, one seemed to point in a different direction to the other. 'Make that your last drink,' slurred Tisha, before turning to go back to the bar.

'You too, and say thanks from me,' she called, as Tisha sashayed away to re-join MacIntosh. By the end of their night at the pub, outside waiting for Sasha's mum, it was the older sister who threw up everywhere. Bea looked on slightly aghast, thinking to herself, *that's weird, I feel brilliant.*

When Christmas arrived, their mum kept it secret when she collected food donations from one of the three food banks in otherwise wealthy Lewes. Sandy was relieved she could scrape enough together so they could all enjoy a bit extra. She still had to work, a busy time of year for a care and support worker, as well as for chefs and others in the hospitality and catering industry. Brian put in an appearance, just before the big day, still uncertain how Sandy would greet him after their last meeting at the hospital. He arrived to promise he would get belated Christmas presents for them, when he got paid in his new job. He was on his way to work and didn't stay. Apart from Bea, his welcome was lukewarm. He left a temporarily moody house, one of the three sad for her dad, two sorry they hadn't made a better effort, in spite of everything, in the season of goodwill!

Sandy was quiet, and when Bea went upstairs Tisha asked her what she was thinking about. Sandy told her she'd been thinking about her and Brian when they first met. Not as they were in the playground at school, that was different, but when they first started going out together, properly. Brian was a tough scrapper with his mates, no one crossed him. But with her he was gentle, it was a quality in him she really liked. He started training with Crystal Palace. All their mates looked up to him, but there was no arrogance about Brian.

Sandy paused and thought, but left unsaid, *If I'm honest, I was the one big-headed about it. I was the one going out with him.*

At Tisha's prompting she continued. 'He was good looking and everything about him promised fun and energy. I remember having our photo taken together for the local newspaper, celebrating the latest teenage football prodigy with his lovely girlfriend. That was before the massive money entered the game, but we still enjoyed a good lifestyle, married at twenty with you on the way.'

Tisha smiled. She'd never heard her mum speak like this before.

There was a lengthy pause. 'You know, every time he left to play a match, the last thing that we'd say was, *Love you forever*, each to the other.' Sandy gave a sigh. Tisha came over and hugged her mum.

Sandy quietly reflected that she had never known another man. The truth was, she didn't know about him. Christmas came and went.

On the last day of the break, Bea called for Alana. From her house they set off for Jack's. By now, Bea was feeling the odd one out. Jack and Alana had seen a lot of each other over the festive break. In fact, Jack had taken the ticket to the concert that was meant for her. That feeling, the one she couldn't quite articulate flooded back. That dense, shadowy, dynamic inside she couldn't find words for. She was pretty sure it wasn't Jack or Alana's intention to make her feel apart from them, then why did it bug her so much? And, even though she tried to think sensibly about it, she began to take some kind of peculiar pleasure in differences with Alana, like a kid picking at a scab.

Bea always loved taking Petra to the Priory to gallop about, but this afternoon felt different. She tried hard to hide her feelings, telling herself the problem was hers, she had to own it. When they got to the green, Jack placed the ball in the hurling device and launched it. Petra sped off in pursuit. Returning with the ball in her smiley mouth, she set it gently upon Jack's lap. If a conversation was in progress Petra joined in, a deep-throated, impatient muttering growl, trying to hasten the next launch. And so on, until finally the exhausted dog collapsed before the throne, chewing at the ball clutched in her paws.

Bea noticed how Alana kept touching Jack, a hand on the shoulder, or a playful slap when Jack said something outrageous. And that's how things were until she learned Alana was staying to have tea at Jack's that evening. Despite doing her best to fight the truth, the reality seeped in that she didn't want to share Alana, not just with Jack, but with anyone. The thing she was feeling, she decided, was conflict. Bea knew that working out her complicated feelings for her friend was a priority if she was to understand her emotions. When the light began to fade they walked back from the Priory, but by that time Bea had become aware Alana had gone quiet. She was curious. When they turned into Jack's street, the silence between all three was plain, even awkward.

Alana said, 'Jack, I think I'm going to have to go home. I've been fighting it, but I feel like I just want to lie down.'

'Okay,' said Jack, with obvious disappointment.

'Can you apologise to your mum for me? I don't know, but I feel crazy tired.'

'Sure I will. Are you coming down with something?'

'I don't know. It feels like nothing I can explain.'

So Alana stood with her head down while Bea opened the door for Jack, who seemed embarrassed. The girls didn't go in. She knew she should have sympathy with her best friend, and felt uncomfortable for taking pleasure in the cancelled tea.

As they walked away from Jack's, Bea asked, 'What do you think's wrong with you?'

Alana said, 'I really don't know. Honestly, there's nothing I can compare it to…it's, like, I have to lie down, but it's more than tired. I don't know.'

Bea couldn't help it, deliberately making herself feel worse as they walked on, unable to stop herself trying to pick an argument. 'It must be bad, for you to act like that. If I know her, Jack's mum would have prepared stuff especially.' When Alana didn't respond Bea turned the screw, 'Although, it seems to be getting a bit of a habit with you, letting people down. As you get older you get more selfish.'

'Please, Bea, I can't do this. Can you just leave it?'

'It's, like, in the summer, you know I needed you.'

'Needed me? Alana queried softly.

'I asked you to help me wash the cars. You couldn't be bothered.'

'Oh, that.'

'Yes, that, Alana, that's what I mean about you.' But Alana didn't respond, and Bea, in spite of noticing the colour had drained from her face, didn't turn off to walk her sick friend home. 'See you in school,' she said, as they parted miserably. If Alana replied, Bea didn't hear her.

14

She was standing a couple of meters in front of the goal and a coach, dressed in a smart Lewes FC track-suit, was lifting footballs from a pool of them in front of him, tossing them to Bea one after another after another. She danced on tip-toe, striking each one as it came to her. Right foot, left foot, right foot. This exercise improved agility, aiming to connect with the ball at the perfect angle to volley past the goalkeeper. Or at least that was the intention. Only there was no goalkeeper for this exercise. It was purely about timing, but Bea's timing was less than perfect. The coach called, 'You're not concentrating.'

Bea, even to her own surprise, burst into tears.

'Whoa. Bea?'

'I'm sorry. It's not you. It's—'

'Let's wrap it up. We can talk if you want.'

Bea wiped her eyes with the back of her hands. 'No. I'll be okay. I think I'll just do a few laps on my own.'

'If you're sure. I have to stay with the others, but you know how to find me if I can help.'

Bea lapped the Convent Fields alone, without a ball at her feet. She just ran, churning things over. The effort of running released endorphins. She had read about them, a naturally occurring chemical substance produced in the brain through energetic exercise. The process helped relieve the sadness in her. Alana hadn't appeared for the start of the new term, neither had she answered Jack's texts. She hadn't answered anyone's texts. By the end of the week, Mrs Winks made an announcement to the class. She wanted everyone to know that Alana was unwell, and may be away for some time. No person in school knew any more than this. Bea was upset and still too embarrassed to call at Alana's house because of the way they'd parted and the things she'd said on the evening they'd left Jack's. She couldn't stop recalling the disloyal way she'd treated Alana, and kept replaying her thoughts and comments when Alana had announced she was unwell: *How could I do that? Why did I think like that?* Running or not, endorphins or not, she had to talk to someone.

At home, Bea waited until Tisha went to her room, and then sat down on the sofa next to her mum. 'Mum, you know that Alana's not at school, and she's sick?'

Sandy turned, but, as soon as their eyes met, Bea began to sob. Unable to speak, she moved closer and flung her arms round her mother's neck. The pair hugged, and Sandy rubbed Bea's back. 'Hey, what is it? What's this about?'

Sandy could feel Bea's whole body judder with waves of successive heavy sobs. Whilst this was going on Tisha came down for something or other, but immediately withdrew back upstairs without a word. It was a minute or two before Bea could form her words.

'Now, when you're ready,' said Sandy.

Bea began to describe her last meeting with Alana, speaking in broken sentences between great involuntary quakes. 'I was awful to her, and I don't know why,' she sputtered.

'Why? What did you say?'

'It's not just that. It's not so much what I said. It's…I was glad she felt bad.'

'You didn't mean it, Bea.'

'But that's just it. I did at the time, and I hate myself for it. It's been a week now. She's not answering anyone's messages or calls, and no one's heard anything from her. I can't wait to say sorry.'

'Then the sooner you do, the better. If she's not back at school soon, you'll have to call at the house.'

The school's first match of the new term was welcomed by Bea more than anything. Preparing for the game, she was extra methodical. Jack had turned her on to an article about living in the moment. Bea found she was fortunate in developing a natural knack of focusing firmly on a task at hand, with an ability to separate out unwanted thoughts. She wondered if this was as easy for everyone, or was it something that she simply had a natural aptitude for? So many of the kids at school seemed stressed, part of growing up, adjusting, hormones engaged, she supposed. She was no different to her peers, but this new focus helped. It was fine to plan, have aspirations and hopes ahead, but fully focusing on the task at hand, whether it was homework, or washing a car, she found could be therapeutic. In bed at night, Bea began to count her blessings, repeating Jack's mantra *make the best of what's been done to you*.

The morning of the match Bea took the medal from under her pillow. She slid it into the pocket cut into the boot, raised the boot, kissed it, and said to herself, '*Believe*.' She placed the boots into her bag. This, then, was the little ritual she had developed before games, but to perform it in the dressing room would invite awkward looks from her teammates. With her rapid improvement, *Getgo* had soon moved her to play up front for the school. Now, it was unusual if Bea didn't score in a match! She'd become prolific and the regular touchline spectators had also noticed a new quality about Bea on the ball. She looked different. She played differently. Her stamina and running allowed her to tackle back, to win the ball in her own half without being out of puff. Hard work in training, whether with others or slogging on her own had rid her of the labouring that had let her body down in games.

Despite playing well, the Brighton opposition were a slick lot; what football people who know, call *technically* very good. Conversely, her team couldn't feed Bea the balls she needed to get near the opposition goal, so she spent much of the match in or near her own half. No place for a goal-scoring centre-forward. Nevertheless, almost every time she did receive the ball Bea was able to show her style. That, allied to her new work rate, attracted the comments of the regular touchline onlookers. Today there was an unfamiliar face in the gathering. A person who walked back and forth wearing an inscrutable expression, who moved from one touchline to the other. Anyone who cared to look away from the game would have observed this person, watching and scribbling in a notebook.

After the match Bea walked back to the school changing rooms, happy for the small mercy of a mild late afternoon. As they entered, the players met the familiar scent of pine disinfectant mingled with sweat. By now the odour failed even to register with most of them. Bea never showered at school, preferring to shower at home when she could take her time and relax afterwards. She sat for a minute to catch her breath, chew over the game and share in the moans about lack of chances created for the forwards. As was the norm in a 2-0 defeat, any defeat, the defenders were unusually quiet. Bea changed out of her boots and placed them in her bag. She slipped on her warm jacket and called goodbye to the team. Then just as she opened the door, a voice yelled, 'Have you heard from Alana?'

'No,' she shouted back, not stopping on her way out.

Bea climbed the steps of the bridge across the railway leading to Court Road and home. It was typical, when her mind wasn't focused her thoughts were on Alana. How much longer would it be before someone told them something? Each day that went by the tension escalated. What was happening? What was she doing? Where was Alana? When she reached home, it was the first thing she mentioned to Tisha.

'If you don't know, you'll have to go round there,' Tisha responded. 'What the hell's happened between you two anyway?'

Bea said nothing about her confused feelings around Alana and Jack. *How can I? I can't explain them to myself.* But she offloaded her sadness, by confessing to her sister the same as she had told her mum. How she had bullied Alana when she was unwell. Now, something awful had happened and she wasn't there for her friend.

Tisha told her, 'I have to say I'm surprised Bea. You know what you have to do.'

On her way back from Jack's the following day, Bea at last summoned the courage to call at Alana's. It was going on for nearly three weeks, and still Alana had not answered her phone to anyone. Mrs Lane opened the door to her.

'Bea! Lovely to see you. Come in. Happy belated New Year.'

She was heartened by the welcome, but still a little embarrassed. Would Mrs Lane ask her why it had taken so long? She didn't. Bea thought she looked tired, and sat down as Mrs Lane pointed to an easy chair. There was no sign of Alana. Bea still hadn't settled on what she was going to say to her. *I can start by saying sorry.* She sat facing the conservatory beyond, thinking the same thought she had many times; how the living room was quite small for the house of a family who were so well off. But there was only Alana, no brothers or sisters, so… Whilst thinking all this Bea's eyes were drawn to the portrait photograph on top of a sky-blue painted bookcase in one corner, Alana and her parents. She started to explain why she hadn't called earlier, but Alana's mum interrupted her.

'Look,' said Mrs Lane, 'I know you guys are all wondering what's happened. The truth is the last few weeks have been so busy, and, as they say, time has flown. We haven't had a minute.'

Mrs Lane stopped suddenly, seeing the serious look on Bea's face, her eyes fixed on the door. This made her sit forward. With her hands clasped as if in prayer, she said softly, 'I have to tell you, Bea, Alana isn't here.'

15

Brian Bagshot had worked flat out over Christmas, without doubt the hotel's busiest time of year. Brian welcomed working again. He'd enjoyed preparing food from as far back as he could remember. Training to become a chef was suggested to him when he had to finish football. He achieved a lot quickly at first and passed examinations, but struggles with the mental side of quitting the game continued to bug him. Alcohol or other drugs were never his bag, but he found the dubious buzz he got from gambling was the nearest he could achieve to the highs he experienced in football. It came nowhere near, of course, in reality. How he wished he'd never taken easy money from his so-called mates who'd never done an honest day's work.

By mid-January he called with late presents and some money for the girls. He asked if he could take everyone out for a meal sometime? Sandy said she'd think about it, but without any enthusiasm, and that was the way things were left. Brian had a lot of trust to regain, at least as far as Sandy and Tisha were concerned. The longer time went on the less able, or willing, the family had been to challenge him about Gramps. Partly, he knew, they feared what they might find out, but his father was happy, things appeared to be relatively comfortable between the pair of them living in the flat, and he hoped that Bea was over the phone fiasco. At least it seemed to him that she'd pushed that humiliation to the end of the line in her list of emotional episodes. He really wanted his girls to be happy.

That evening was a night off work for Brian. He took the opportunity to explain to Gramps what he had said to the police, and what they said to him. He had charges to face, likely to go to court. The pair sat facing one another. The television was on, which made it easier for Brian.

'Dad, what can I say about what happened? I told them I was finished with them and wasn't scared of them. So they got at me by getting at you. What they did to you was my punishment as well for not doing what they wanted.'

Brian was staying with Gramps for two reasons, for his own peace of mind that the old man was not living alone, *and* he wanted a better more settled life, not just for him. As if guessing the thoughts running through his head, his dad asked, 'What *do* you actually want?'

'I'm a failure in life…in love…I want my girls back, my family back. You know I just couldn't cope when I had to finish at Palace, when I had to finish full stop, Dad.'

'For god's sake, Brian, that was almost ten years ago. The girls are more mature than you. It's sad enough that you still haven't found what you're looking for, even sadder that you don't *know* what you're looking for.'

Brian fidgeted in the chair and told Gramps that the hotel owner was a Palace fan who actually remembered him playing. 'I ran into a fella I used to know from catering college who suggested I phone the hotel to see if he'd speak to me, and things moved from there. He's a bit of a mouthpiece, but he's alright I suppose. He's rich.'

'Does he know about the business with the police?'

'I've told him everything. That's why I think I can make it. He's willing to keep me on, wants to send me on courses, even speak for me at court if it comes to it. I just need a break, Dad, and I think this is it. Life's been a bit chaotic for me, that's all. It's all well and good for you—'

'I try to live life according to my conscience, what I feel inside is right.'

'You had Mum's support, she—'

'Leave your mother out of this. You'd have had all the support you needed from Sandy. The trouble is she couldn't find you to support you. You weren't there. You need to speak to her, p'raps you *can* make it up with her, but it'll take time. This ain't going to happen overnight. You can stay with me as long as you like, that'll save you a bit and you could settle yourself. I don't want any money off you.'

Brian started to become emotional. This was the most intimate conversation they'd had in years, perhaps ever. 'I'm sorry I couldn't help when Mum died. I was in a bad place. I don't have any excuse.' Silence, then Brian added, 'She would have loved the walks round here.'

'She came to hate London. She spent her life in hospitals, doing what she thought was right, helping other people. She worked all her life in 'em, and then died in one.'

They fell silent again, then Gramps said, 'This life can work for you, son, when you realise what you've got. We're all on a journey. We all get highs 'n' lows. Have you quit gambling?'

'Yeah.'

'Right you are. Now, wake up!'

There was a knock at the door, a pause and then the noise of a key in the door. Bea appeared. The two men switched their intense conversation and greeted her with broad smiles.

The smiles were not returned. 'Hi, I've just finished my tea at Jack's. I saw your bike, Dad, and thought I'd say hello.'

Despite her sullen look, Gramps said, 'Just in time to make us a cup o' tea, we're gasping.'

'I'm surprised at you, Gramps. I thought you were better than that. Times have moved on. Your able-bodied son's here now. He can make the tea.'

Gramps cleared his throat, 'Sorry, I was forgetting decades of old school. I have to be a new man. Brian.'

Brian jumped up, gave Bea a quick hug, and marched out to put the kettle on. 'I'm a new man,' he muttered disappearing into the kitchen.

Bea sat next to Gramps with her serious look and gave him a peck on his cheek. She studied his face, noted the fading marks.

'What're you looking so down about?' he asked. 'Tell me.'

She ignored his question. 'How's the knee? Are you still using the neoprene mum got you?'

'Indeed I am, and us two walked over to Grange Gardens. The trees and flowers are all sleeping, but it's still full of colour.' In a weak attempt to cheer her up, he said, 'I was talking to a squirrel who said to say hello to you.'

Bea failed to respond. They sat in silence until Brian came through carrying three mugs of tea in one fist, and put them on the coffee table in front of Gramps. A mouth-watering scent from the kitchen wafted in along with him.

'Oh, what's that cooking?' said Bea, breathing in, but still with a straight face.

Pretending to be the world's greatest cook, Brian said, 'Just a little something I threw together.'

'Seriously Dad.'

'Stroganoff,' he said. 'You going to join us?'

'I can't, but I'd love to, smells great.'

'Your daughter's in serious training now, son. Can't you tell?'

'You look great,' Brian said. 'But then you always did.'

'Hmm. Maybe I did, but I can run and run now without feeling my lungs are going to burst.'

'So,' said Gramps, 'We can see you're down. I want to hear it.'

Bea took a deep breath, and let out a sigh. She looked at the floor, then from one to the other, and began slowly, 'You know my friend, Alana? She's my *bestie*, we play football. Gramps knows her. Well, I think she's very sick, she's in hospital.'

'Poor girl,' said Gramps. 'Go on.'

'Not only that, but…well, before all this, the last time I saw her we had a row. That is, we didn't row exactly, it was me…I wasn't very nice to her.' Bea's eyes welled up, 'I'm worried about her, and I'm so unhappy because I was horrible to her.'

'What if I take you up to see her?' said Brian. 'Where is she?'

Bea sniffed and wiped her eyes with the backs of her hands.

'Go and get a tissue, Brian,' instructed Gramps. Brian got up and looked about.

'She's been having tests, but they still don't know what's wrong. Her mother hopes she'll be home next week. We did everything together. We joined Lewes, Alana and me.' Then she hesitated.

'Carry on, Bea,' said Brian, coming back and handing over a wad of tissues. 'Is there anything we can do?'

'I just don't want her to die,' said Bea, breaking down completely and covering her face with her hands.

The two men felt useless, each thinking desperately what they could do. Brian knelt beside his daughter, but it was her Gramps she wanted. The old man sensed it. He struggled out

120

of his chair and went to her. Bea immediately stood up and they hugged. They hugged for a long time, while Brian sat down, forlorn. He watched them, leaning forward with his hands on his knees, waiting.

'Right, this is a big deal that none of us knows how to fix just now,' said Gramps at last, patting Bea's back. 'Until, in good time, when things will unfold, all we can do is let them play out, natural like. So come on, come and sit down.'

They sat in silence, the two men feeling her pain, as Bea slowly began to recover. In a minute she gave her nose a good strong blow. Much to their relief, she started to talk and picked up where she left off.

'Alana and me, we joined Lewes, and I started a really, like, serious training programme, Dad, supervised by the club's coaches.'

'I nearly got in trouble over it,' Gramps said, looking at Brian.

'They played me up front. That's where I've always wanted to play. You know that. Then, after that, the school played me up front. Now, it's where I play, scoring *bagshots* of goals for the Under16s,' she said, with a sniff and a weak laugh.

'Bagshots of goals, very funny,' said Brian.

'I'm sorry I haven't got to see you yet,' added Gramps. 'I just don't think the old knee would hold up in the cold.'

'That's okay,' she said.

The emotion in the room had still not completely settled when Bea's phone beeped. She stood up and lifted it from her jacket, slung over the back of a chair. Brian glanced at his father, both imagining what the other was thinking about the phone fiasco. Brian took himself to the bathroom as Bea answered, 'Hello.'

'Hi Bea, it's Jacqui from Lewes FC. I know it's getting late, but I've got someone with me from Brighton…that's Brighton & Hove Albion. He's wondering if we could call round, to speak to you and your mum if it's convenient, tonight? Sorry about the short notice. It doesn't have to be tonight obviously, but it would be handy. Is your mum there? Hello?'

Bea couldn't speak. Her head whirred like a rogue drone, her mouth felt dry and her heart pounded. She looked at her Gramps and took a breath, finally managing to stammer a reply. 'Uh, I don't know Jacqui…uh, I'm not at home. I mean, I'm at my grandad's. Can you tell me what this is about? I mean, what do they want?'

'Right. Well I can tell you it's about your football, obviously, and I suppose they want to speak to you and your mum about any thoughts you have for the future.'

Despite a thrill at hearing this, Bea suddenly felt drained. She had explored the guilt she felt over Alana's situation with everyone closest to her, but she still felt sensitive, as though she couldn't face something this evening that was likely to demand more decision-making from her. 'I don't know what to say, Jacqui. Things are happening tonight. Would it be alright to make it another night?'

'Okay, that's okay. Perhaps we'd better make it another time?'

'Yeah. I think that's best. Like, I'm not sure what's happening tonight,' Bea laughed nervously.

'Sorry, this is all a bit out of the blue for you, it's just that he was in Lewes and called me. Obviously someone from Brighton has watched you play and wants to speak to you and your mum. But it's too short notice, I understand. I can tell him they'll have to make it another time. I guess we might be losing you.'

A still shocked Bea wasn't sure she'd said *Bye*, before the call was suddenly ended. Brian came back in. He gathered up the empty mugs and walked through to the kitchen. When the three were in the room again, Bea told them what her call had been about.

'That's fantastic,' said Gramps. 'Come here 'til I hug you.'

'That's marvellous news,' said Brian, awkwardly resting his hand on her shoulder whilst Gramps and Bea hugged.

Bea sat down in silence, beginning to feel embarrassed by the pair staring at her with a wide grin apiece. She felt worn-out and was slumped in an armchair with her legs crossed straight out in front of her, her fingers joined on her lap like a mediaeval monk in prayer.

'In other circumstances this would almost call for a *cebralation*,' said Gramps, deliberately fuddling his words in the way only he thought funny. 'As I say, things will unfold, and all we can do is wait to see what they bring.'

Bea hugged Dad and Gramps and left the cheap modern flats to walk home through the ages reflected in the ancient buildings along the street. She looked up on a cold, clear night to catch a shooting star. For a few moments she was exhilarated, it was good news, promising news, but then cautioned herself against feeling too self-satisfied – Alana. She questioned as she walked whether lives were already mapped out for everyone. Some people believed that even if we still had to make things happen, *agency* they called it, ultimately our destinies were written in the stars. This made her think back to when she was a child, when she heard on the news of a little boy, no more than a baby really, who'd been washed up on a beach. His parents were fleeing from war. She had cried, and remembered mum consoling her. Even now she remembered the little boy's name. Could that really have been his destiny she wondered?

When she reached home she told them about her phone call. Tisha and Sandy could barely contain their delight at the news, yet Bea's thoughts remained elsewhere. In bed, after all the excitement, she couldn't sleep thinking about Alana.

16

Bea was training with the others under the lights. She was trying to learn to love the stretching and warming up sessions before a ball was kicked. She knew she never would. Then the balls were rolled out, and it was *keepie-uppie* time.

A voice called, 'Bea,' and she looked up to receive a pass. It looped from the kicker, coming down at a difficult angle, but she controlled the ball instantly with the inside of her foot. Her movement was accomplished and she felt a surge of pleasure and satisfaction. Flicking the ball to one side, she sprayed a long, low pass, a *daisycutter*. The touch and sound of the ball caressing and leaving her foot was magic. The evening was crisp, breath forming vapour on the cold air. All the players and coaches were laughing, at least before the serious stuff began. *We have fun here, why would I want to leave this?* Bea thought.

When the training session was over, Bea was tired, looking forward to a shower and more so the thought of climbing into her bed. As she called, 'Night, see you,' one of the coaches, wearing a puffa jacket and warm gloves, caught up with her. From under a stout bobble hat, she whispered, 'I hear you're leaving us.'

Bea smiled, 'I don't know. I'll have to wait and see.'

'It's a great opportunity, Bea. You've been scouted! Brighton are interested in you! That's a Premiership club. Anyway, well done, take care, see you!'

Bea checked her phone. There it was, finally, a text from Alana. **Hi B mum sed u called sorry no txt been ill feelin bit better shd be home weekend xx**

Bea was elated and hurried home, thinking how to reply.

As soon as she was through the door she announced to her mum, 'Alana texted, she might be home this weekend.'

'Oh, I'm *sooo* glad for her. Tell me about it, but first d'you want something to eat?'

'Just a snack, Mum, I'm going for a shower first.'

'Tisha's in there.'

'Crap,' said Bea, going upstairs to her room.

She threw her bag in the corner, sat on her bed and texted. **Lan brill. Cant wait t see u SORRY xx All sends luv specially me xx**

She phoned Jack.

'Yeah, she texted me,' he said. 'I had to sit down.'

'Very funny.'

'I know. I'd tell you I wanna be a stand-up comedian, but that one's about fifty years old!'

'Jack, I'm so happy.'

Jack said he was, too, and they discussed how to play it. Bea said she'd speak to Mrs Lane, and see what she said about going round to visit. Ending the call, she heard Tisha come out of the bathroom.

'Did Mum tell you?' she called to Bea. 'Someone's coming round to see you tomorrow.'

That week Brian didn't start work until late afternoons. He walked in to his solicitor's office for his 10 am appointment feeling confident. Brian hoped that when this business was over, eventually Sandy and the girls would accept him back to live with them. He wanted to have done with his co-defendants, those responsible for the attack against Gramps, once and for all. If his part in the mobile phones wrongdoing could be separated from theirs, with luck it would leave him only facing a charge of Handling Stolen Goods. His solicitor, a man with ruddy cheeks and a goatee beard, told him, 'If the court agrees, your case will be adjourned for Probation reports.'

'What? That means all this'll drag on,' pleaded Brian.

'Don't forget, Brian, you've got previous for this. A custodial sentence isn't absolutely out of the frame.'

'Jail! You're not serious?'

'It's your record, Brian. Okay, it's not the worst in the world, but that's where the Probation Officer comes in, to suggest a community-based option as an alternative to custody.'

Brian left feeling less confident about things. Emerging from the building he was confronted by the betting shop directly opposite. He crossed the road and stepped inside. He stopped, and stood still to savour the thrill. A familiar excitement coursed through him. The half dozen punters present totally ignored him. He took a betting slip, speed-read the odds in front of him, and scribbled on the slip. He took two twenty pound notes from his pocket, walked to the counter and placed the money down along with the betting slip. The woman tapped a machine and handed him a receipt. No words were spoken, no please, no thank you. He turned, made his way to the door and left, hating himself.

As they waited for their visitor, Bea and Sandy sat on the sofa watching telly. Tisha was upstairs getting ready to go out. She wouldn't tell them where she was going, all they knew was someone was coming to pick her up.

'You seem relaxed,' said Sandy.

'I am,' Bea replied.

'Thought you would've been all excited.'

As Bea shrugged, there was a knock at the door. Sandy sprang up to answer it, realising she was more excited than Bea.

A woman. Dressed in a smart blue tracksuit under a rain jacket. 'Ms Bagshot?'

'Oh, I was expecting a man,' Sandy said and laughed at herself. 'Yes, sorry, hello, come in, please.'

'I'm Geraldine,' the woman said, stepping into the hallway and handing over an ID card that identified her as a member of AITC - *Albion in the Community*. Sandy took her coat, placed it over the stairs and guided her into the living room.

Bea stood up and as she shook Geraldine's hand she felt a burst of nervous excitement, and a thought occurred to her. Sandy was offering the guest coffee or tea when Bea said, 'Umm, can you give me one moment. I, eh… I need to go to the bathroom. Excuse me, Geraldine. Sorry, I'll be straight back.'

She galloped upstairs and went straight into her room, threw back her pillow and grasped the magic medal. Placing it in her pocket she detoured to the bathroom. Delaying for a moment, she gazed at herself in the mirror and her hand played over the contour of the medal through her jeans. A feeling overcame her that she couldn't explain. Not nervousness, not panic, like she thought she might feel, but a calming sense of composure she had rarely felt before. Yes, it was still tinged with excitement on its outer edges, but it was different. She gave a last smile to the mirror, flushed the loo and went back downstairs full of confidence.

By the time Sandy returned with the coffees, Geraldine had learned that Bea liked school, had just turned fifteen, her dad used to play for Crystal Palace, but that he didn't live with them.

'You'll have guessed by now,' said Geraldine, speaking to Sandy, 'that we've been watching Bea play football, and we'd like to invite her...' She stopped and turned to Bea. 'Sorry, we'd like to invite *you* to join us at Brighton.'

'Our Girls' Player Pathway has various programmes, I won't bore you with the aspects of all them for now, but we really do believe you could go straight into our advanced training centre. This is aimed at girls like you, under-16s, and the sessions take place at Brighton & Hove Albion's elite football performance centre, in Lancing. The centre is designed to bring together the best regional players into an environment that challenges and encourages their further development.' Geraldine paused and took a sip of her coffee. Bea beamed a smile at her mum. Sandy worked hard to stifle a nervous giggle at what she was hearing.

Geraldine continued, 'It's a smaller player to coach ratio that champions our academy philosophy. Bea, from what our scouts have reported and from what I have seen myself watching you with Lewes, I think you'd progress quite quickly to the final tier of the AITC pathway. It sits directly below Brighton & Hove Albion's own academy structure. Places on the AITC are only available to girls who have been formally invited through our scouting network, and we'd like to invite you. In simple terms, we want you to join us.' Geraldine stopped talking and reached for her coffee again.

Sandy looked towards Bea, but her daughter was quiet. Smiling, but quiet. 'What do *you* think, Bea?' she asked.

'Lancing's a long way. I'm not sure how I'd get there.'

Sandy took a moment. This was not what she'd expected. She thought Bea would've been over the moon with delight. Instead, Bea's comment had been voiced in a measured tone.

'Well, I'm sure we could work out travel arrangements, Bea. I think there may be one or two older girls from this area who go back and forth.'

Before anyone could say anything more, Tisha belted down the stairs, popped her head round the door, nodded at the woman from AITC and announced she was off out. Sandy couldn't resist going to the window. When the car turned she thought she recognised the man driving. She gaped, just a fraction too long, until she collected herself and sat back down.

'Sorry. Daughters!' she said to Geraldine who smiled in agreement. 'Could we come and see what exactly this all entails?'

'Of course, that won't be a problem. I'm sure you'll want to know about safeguarding and how that operates for the welfare of the young people who come under our duty of care.'

Sandy nodded and turned to Bea, 'Well, what do you say?'

'I'd like to think about it,' Bea answered, adding to Sandy's amazement.

'Of course you do. We completely understand that.' Geraldine took a business card from her purse and placed it on the table in front of them. 'Have a think, talk it over, and let us know what you decide.' She stood, and Bea and Sandy stood too. Sandy saw her to the door.

As Geraldine put her coat on and stepped outside, she added, 'It's a great opportunity you know.'

'I know,' Sandy said.

Returning to the living room, she smiled at her daughter. 'Bea?' Bea's face was inscrutable. 'I thought you'd be over the moon.'

'I am, Mum, in a way.'

'Well then? What's the matter?'

'I play for Lewes,' said Bea. Something made her feel, more strongly than she'd ever felt anything, that it wasn't time for her to make a change. Yet added to that was the confidence that overflowed inside her simply from the evening's visit. She had been scouted. She was wanted by a Premiership setup. Her rising self-confidence was like an unstoppable surge.

In the car Tisha turned to MacIntosh. Sadly, it wasn't the MacIntosh of the pub, or the one behind the witty texts he had sent her. Perhaps it was because he was driving, but Tisha was confronted with the MacIntosh of their first meeting. He might have been off duty, but he was DC MacIntosh once again.

'Speak to me, baby,' she teased. 'Where are we heading?'

'I thought we could go for drive.'

'Uh, *hello*, it's dark.'

'Yes. Obviously we can call in somewhere as well.'

'It's *pitch* dark.'

'Well, where would you like to go?'

'I thought you were taking me out?' she said.

He stammered.

Tisha faced forward. 'We should have arranged this better.'

'Yes, I suppose…what would you have chosen then?'

'I dunno. Komedia, or somewhere.'

They fell into an uneasy quiet until they parked up in Brighton and set out to find a place to eat. She wished they could go for a drink, because that seemed the only way he could possibly liven up…but he would have to drive her home, so that was a non-starter. They plumped for a Chinese, where he decided he could allow himself a small beer.

131

'I shouldn't really,' he said. 'You never know, even one could send you over the limit.'

'But you're a policeman. They wouldn't do anything to you.'

'Uh, that's not the way it works, I'm afraid.'

'Why don't you have a few low or no alcohol beers? I've heard people say it tricks the brain into thinking you've had a real drink, but wouldn't affect your driving ability!'

'Hmm, I don't think it'd work that way on my brain, besides I've tried it, awful stuff,' he said pulling a face and then blushing.

Tisha was desperate to get the man to relax. 'My dad,' she said at last. 'How d'you think that's going to go?'

'I can't discuss that. Sorry. It'd be unprofessional.'

'What if you *were* unprofessional, just for an itsy-bitsy moment? Could you discuss it then?'

MacIntosh let out a nervous laugh. 'I think not.'

'What about me then? You met me in the course of your work. What would the top man think of that?'

MacIntosh said, 'That's different, you weren't a suspect nor, strictly speaking, helping police inquiries. Fact is, we met in a pub when I was off duty.' He clearly wanted to change the subject, but he didn't say anything else.

Tisha took a breath. Sport, surely that would work. 'Do you like football?' she asked.

'I can take it or leave it.'

'Well, what music do you like?'

'Classical actually.'

'Apart from chatting up pretty girls in pubs, what else do you do off duty? Any hobbies?'

'Umm…not really.'

'Wow boy! Where's the charmer who talked me round in circles gone?' Tisha said and smiled to lessen the severity of her comment.

MacIntosh conceded that a few drinks, 'takes me out of myself.'

'I've always thought that a curious expression, y'know, as if we're all two-faced.'

'Ah, now, there *is* an interesting point,' he said and his face brightened. 'Several philosophers have—'

'Do you know what?' Tisha interrupted. 'Why don't we leave philosophy to another time? Give us something to look forward to,' said Tisha exasperated. 'Not just now while we're eating. P'raps next time?'

It turned out MacIntosh was a sweet man but, even, as she learnt, with a degree in Philosophy, he was a little out of his depth.

Tisha wondered to herself, *why do some people need alcohol to oil their social wheels?*

17

With her homework finished, Bea was lying on her bed going over the meeting with the woman from AITC.

Despite the tremendous offer, Bea wanted to continue with Lewes where she'd started to make her name playing up front. The people were friendly and made her feel welcome. Would the performance centre at Lancing really be a step up, or only a side step? Then there would be the travelling back and forth. How would that work? How much would that cost? Gramps might be able to help, but she couldn't expect mum to, yet mum hadn't questioned the cost of travel. She seemed to be all for it.

Bea twisted onto her side. Then back again, staring up at the ceiling. No, her ambition now was to play for Lewes, the Women's first team. She knew it would take a few years and guessed she couldn't play for them even if she was good enough, not until she was at least seventeen or eighteen and had left school.

But she had doubts. One thing Bea couldn't work out was, if Brighton & Hove Albion had offered her this, then why hadn't Lewes, *my club*, offered the same? Were they unsure she was good enough to progress in the Girl's Development Squad? Bea determined to speak to *Getgo* tomorrow at school, to see what he thought. She got ready for bed and went to clean her teeth. Downstairs, she heard Tisha come in and her mind cast back to the time they enjoyed before Christmas, the wonderful evening in Brighton. She shuddered remembering Tisha throwing up at the end of the night. As she cleaned her teeth, Bea pondered how common it was for people to be sick after drinking too much. She'd heard it talked about like it was almost the norm. She wondered what made her so different? It hadn't affected her. She thought to herself how exciting it would be to go out and enjoy another night like that sometime.

Next morning Bea joined the side yard footballers, deciding to say nothing about her good fortune in being scouted. Most players with ability got carried away with their prowess and good luck, but not Bea. Her modesty and lack of arrogance, as her football reputation increased, had begun to draw a quiet admiration from most of the kids at school. She realised it at the same time she realised there was no longer any mileage for the models to take their unhappiness out on her. Apart from that time she'd stupidly attacked Clarkson, she had always tried to ignore them. Now her self-confidence could let any of their taunts bounce off her. It wasn't always so easy for other kids, an observation that wasn't lost on Bea. What had definitely been lost was the reason she'd been called *Beefy*, although, despite the change in body shape, the tag remained in use with her school teammates! *To me Beef, Pass!*

At break time, Bea stopped *Getgo*, asking if he had a minute to spare. She explained she was a little confused about her recent offer and wondered where she stood with Lewes.

'To tell the truth, Bea, we've been slow off the mark, but your skills have rocketed in a whirlwind of time. I've never seen anything quite like it, must all be down to those new boots of yours!' he joked. 'Since you've been sporting those luminous green boots you've been a scoring sensation.'

'Do you think there's a chance I could be included in, and train with, the development squad?'

'Whoa, hold on girl! That's practically the first team reserves. I mean you are advancing quickly, but don't forget, those development squad girls are at least seventeen years old. Most older.'

'But—'

Getgo held up his hand to stop her. 'Look Bea, I think people at the club see you having fun and enjoying yourself, and above all they want to be careful about things. The worst possible thing they could do is heap pressure on you. Football careers have been ruined by the pressure of expectation.'

'But why haven't Lewes made an offer?' Bea finally managed to ask.

'Truthfully, the fact Brighton have come in for you, a Premiership club, means that everyone at Lewes thought it only fair not to try and obstruct them approaching you. We want you to enjoy your football, but we couldn't and wouldn't want to limit opportunities for you. But if you are asking, then I believe Lewes would prefer you to stay. Actually, I know they'd love you to stay.'

At the end of the school day, she and Jack met in the yard to walk home. In Alana's absence Jack had seen the sense of the more direct route to his house, along Southover High Street. The talk was about Alana's impending return home that weekend.

Jack asked, 'If she does, will you arrange with her mum for us to call round?'

'Of course, I'll give Mrs Lane a call tonight to see if she knows what's happening. How serious do you think things must be?'

'She's been in hospital how long now, three weeks? We'd better not speculate until Alana tells us what she knows. That is *if* she knows anything.'

'If *she* doesn't, who does?'

'Bea, one thing you're forgetting is, we may have more sense than a lot of so-called adults, but doctors and parents will still treat us the way they think kids have to be treated!'

'Fuck's sake. We're not kids.'

'There's something else I need to tell you,' Jack said, 'although I've been told to mind my own business.'

'I'm all ears.'

'You know your mum was round ours the other night?'

'I didn't know. No.'

'Well, your mum and mine were talking, and I happened to stop outside the door.'

'Spying, nice,' Bea said.

'No, not spying. I was looking for Petra who'd wandered off because I was ignoring her. Anyway, your mum was saying that your dad wants you all to join him and go to live in Brighton. He wants to get a house there, near to the hotel where he works.'

Bea raised her face to the sky and felt a pull of frustration. 'And? What else?'

'Your mum was saying, like, there was no way she was going to uproot you from school now you're doing so well and everything. So I wondered...' he paused.

Bea looked down to him. 'What?'

'How did you keep it from her that you're the thickest in the class?'

'Not funny, Jack. Now go on, what else was said?'

'Nothing. Petra came to the door sniffing and wagging her tail like she usually does, so I was discovered and accused of eavesdropping. Then it was, like, *anything said here stays here*. Does your dad know about the Brighton scout?'

'He couldn't, she was only round last night. Oh, now I think of it, he knew about the phone call I got because we were at Gramps' flat. Of course, I told them about it. I didn't think Dad and Mum were speaking, so that's new. I wonder when that was.'

'Don't drop me in it anyway,' said Jack, as they reached the house.

They heard the familiar sniff-sniff coming from behind the door. Bea opened it with Jack's keys and they both enjoyed the usual waggy-smiley greeting.

'Tea's ready when you are,' called Janis.

Bea hadn't intended to call with Gramps that evening, but she decided to look in, armed with the information supplied by Jack.

'Hi Gramps! Dad at work?'

'Hello my darling, didn't expect you tonight. Is everything alright?'

'All good Gramps. That scout, from the phone call the other night, she was round to speak to me.'

Bea told Gramps about the conversation with Geraldine, explained her feelings about it, went on to tell him about her talk with *Getgo* earlier that afternoon and said that she thought she would prefer to stay and play her football with Lewes. When she added that Mum seemed to be all for her swapping to Brighton and hadn't even mentioned the cost of travelling to the elite centre at Lancing, she tested the old man.

'What do *you* think Gramps?'

'I couldn't be any more pleased for you, my darling.'

'I mean, I wasn't expecting Mum to be, like, that... like, positive.' Bea was weighing Sandy's response to the scout's invitation against Jack's report that there was no way she was going to uproot her from school. She trusted her mum, but also knew how artful parents could be when they were busy making plans for their kids. She decided to come straight out with it.

'Gramps, do you know anything about Dad wanting us to live together again...to move to Brighton?'

'All I know, Bea, is that your dad told me he wants you all together again, as a family. That's his goal. He says he's got this job now and his boss believes in him. He thinks he can do well, 'specially once this court business is all done with.'

'But has he spoken to Mum about it?'

'If he has, he hasn't told me anything.'

'I always expect you to be straight with me, Gramps.'

'I swear my darling, the talk we had was only the other night, that night you were round and got your phone call.'

'I don't wanna move from Lewes, Gramps,' said Bea, before adding quietly, 'even to be with Dad. My friends are here, you're here. This is where I'm happiest.'

Bea put her arms around Gramps' neck. Each saw the other's eyes moist.

'Go and make us both a cuppa tea,' said the old man.

18

Arriving for training next evening, Bea was met by one of the coaches who told her two representatives from the club were there to see her. She pointed Bea over to the side of the pitch.

'Hi Bea, you know me,' said Jacqui, the woman who had phoned her initially about news of Brighton's interest. 'And this is Karen from the club's board of directors.'

Both women were wrapped up with hats and scarves against the cold, crisp evening. Karen said, 'We were speaking yesterday to Mr Marks. I think you know him better as *Getgo*,' she laughed.

Bea listened as they told her that Lewes hoped she would stay and learn her football with them. 'It would mean you continuing with the *Under 16s* for the present, and perhaps quite soon training with the *Under 18s*. You know that would be a big step up, the girls are obviously older than you and the physicality of the game changes, but we think if you're good enough you're old enough, as they say. It would mean you could get a game for them, but you won't merely be sitting on the side-lines for ever. The under16s will still need you, especially for their Cup run. We understand the attraction of the invite from Albion in the Community and whichever you choose, you'll always be made welcome here, we want you to know that,' Karen said and looked at Jaqui.

'So, what d'you think? Would you like to take some time to consider?' Jacqui asked.

Bea was elated and thanked both women. Her mind was already set. 'I don't need time. I don't want to move from Lewes. This is my home town club and I want to stay. I don't have to think on it anymore.'

The pair seemed delighted and, with them watching on, Bea was electrified in training. The weeks and weeks of running without the ball, of skipping, sit-ups and the rest of the training routine, combined with her new diet, meant that *Beef* was transformed from the puffed out version into a puffed up girl of perpetual motion. Working out on the 3G *Rookery* pitch meant Bea wore her boots and, yet despite the absence of her *Believe* ritual reserved for competitive match-days, she never gave a thought to her outstanding performances in training. Her enthusiasm, talent and skill level didn't suffer. Had she confided that in her Gramps he'd have merely shaken his head and said, 'The superstition of footballers is a crazy affair.'

Bea knocked on Alana's door. Mrs Lane was happy to see her again and welcomed her in. 'Alana is expected to be discharged next weekend,' said Mrs Lane. 'The thing is Bea, you'll find her changed…just a bit.'

'Changed?'

'Yes. I'm telling you now, so that you'll, er…I know you'll be okay when you see her.'

Bea was taken aback by this and looked puzzled. 'You haven't said what's wrong with her. I can tell it's something serious.'

'Alana's still unwell, Bea, just remember that when you see her for the first time. It's worrying us all that the doctors are still uncertain. They've given us a list of what it could be, but they can't say for sure because they don't know themselves. More tests are happening, that's why she's not coming home for another week.'

'Will it be okay for my cousin, Jack Philips, to visit with me as well?'

Mrs Lane hesitated, 'I think not, not for the first visit. And, not on the Saturday she arrives back. We have to work things out. Perhaps a visit on Sunday, on your own would be best.'

Needing to digest what she had heard, Bea decided not to phone Jack right away. On her way home she recalled a happier time. The two were walking and laughing, Alana saying, *It seems like we'll be young forever, but we won't. I think about my health whenever I think about Jack.* Now it's come to this. She thought about all the stuff in her life that made her unhappy, the situation with Dad and Mum, Gramps getting visibly older, her jealousy, witnessing bullying she could never do enough to challenge, the little boy washed up on a beach. Dwelling on each allowed Bea to appreciate her place in the world, her good fortune.

Both Mum and Tisha were there when she got in. The first thing she reported was about calling with Mrs Lane and about Alana.

'What d'you think she meant, Mum?'

Tisha butted in, 'It's pretty obvious isn't it? Alana's sick and her mum's priming you, so you don't freak out when you meet her!'

'I wonder what I can take her on Sunday...to cheer her up?'

Sandy said, 'What does she like? Or why not just tell her all your news the first time? If we can't think of anything, then ask

142

her what you can get her next time you call. See what she wants.'

'I've had only good news since she's been away,' Bea said sadly. 'It makes me feel guilty.'

'Life's like that,' said Tisha.

'I have other news,' Bea said. It was her first opportunity to tell them about staying with Lewes and joining the older girls. She was glad to hear a positive response from her mum. 'I had a feeling you wanted me to join with the Albion thing, that maybe you'd thought about leaving Lewes? Have you discussed it with Dad?'

'Leaving here? What gave you that idea? Your dad and me have had a conversation, but I want you to know your happiness means more to me than anything. I promise that if I discuss with your father anything that directly impacts on you, then you'll know about it.'

Whatever had gone on between her parents, time would have to tell.

Amidst the clatter of the commercial kitchen, Brian Bagshot was on his break talking with his boss, the hotel owner, Aubrey D'Arbay. Brian expressed the pride he felt in Bea, and what was happening for her in the football world. D'Arbay listened with interest. The two men were opposites. The boss was a man full of self-importance, but despite that, it appeared as if he adored Brian. He was a football nut, a season-ticket holder at Crystal Palace, dreaming of making mega-millions which he would use to buy the Premiership football club. Until then he loved being mates with an ex-player, even one most Palace fans had long forgotten. Brian had shown D'Arbay his court summons, and told him he needed to ask for a letter from his employer to present at court alongside the Probation Officer's report.

'I'll have it written on the hotel's best embossed paper,' chirped his boss. 'Things are going to change for you, Brian. We're Palace people you and me. I pride myself on being a superb judge of character, and I know you've got what it takes.'

By the time Brian finished his shift it was midnight. He sped home, fatigued, not thinking of anything much. As he turned into Gramps' road he switched off the bike's engine and freewheeled down along to park outside his father's flat. It wasn't the weekend so most of the dwellings were in darkness.

He parked the bike up and removed his crash helmet. Sitting for a few seconds, he removed his gloves and rubbed a hand across his tired face. He always parked the bike away from the main road, away from the street lighting. No sooner had Brian got off the machine and applied the lock, than three shapes stepped out from the shadows.

On her way to school Bea was charged with that familiar vague feeling she recognised and questioned in herself, but didn't understand. There was no doubt she was looking forward to telling Jack about going to visit Alana on Sunday without him. She wished she didn't hold that feeling, but she did. Like everyone else, she thought, *I'm a work in progress*. That thought held her together for now. After the meeting with Geraldine, Bea convinced herself that she would start to carry the magic medal around with her, safe in her pocket. She'd started to believe the medal on her person lent her greater self-confidence, made her more sure of herself. The conflicts she had experienced over the few short months since her birthday made her think deeply about things, and this encouraged her to link her pact with Gramps to personal issues she faced.

There was no one kicking a ball in the yard this morning, and for once Bea didn't care. It was pouring with rain from an iron grey sky, the sort of morning that welcomed a low mood. Bea, however, was in good form. Her world was as uncertain as the next girl's, but had plenty going for it. Despite the rain, she'd still left the house at her usual early time out of habit to kick a ball about. In fact, she was so early she hadn't spotted one other person in a school uniform. For a moment she considered calling at Jack's and getting a lift back to school with him in his taxi, but it was too wet. Then she saw Mr Evans the caretaker letting a tall wiry boy in. She knew him to see and knew a little about him from the usual school rumour mill; he was only a year ahead of her, but they'd never really spoken, although she knew his nickname was Budgie.

'Hi,' she said. 'Nice day.'

'Hi, Bea,' Budgie replied. 'What's happening with you?'

The pair had never passed the time of day, but she noted he'd called her by name. She was cautious, as she always was at a first meeting, but in tandem with that she felt strangely at ease. Like she had known him and spoken to him for ages before this morning. There was no awkwardness between them. It seemed right to her to mention Alana, given that she guessed the whole school was interested in the welfare of one of their own.

'Nothing much, but Alana Lane's coming out of hospital soon, so I'm looking forward to seeing her.'

'Nice girl, Alana…she starting back?'

'Not yet for a while. I'll visit, see what's happening.'

They hung up their wet coats. Budgie produced a towel from his bag and made to dry his shock of black hair, then stopped and offered the towel to Bea first. 'I saw you two a few weeks back,' he said. 'In town, when those clowns were trying to mess you and Alana around. She twisted his nose. Hilarious.'

'Oh, were you there? We didn't see you. That was so funny.'

More bodies soon piled in to the cloakroom, all soaking wet.

'You box, don't you?' Bea said.

'Yeah. I suppose boxing to me might be what football is to you. I wouldn't mind going for it if I'm good enough. You never fancied doing a Nicola Adams?'

Bea found his voice...what exactly? *Oh!* she thought. She was attracted by Budgie's deep voice. It was the first time she'd noticed how attractive a voice could be.

'I don't think I'd make a good boxer. You don't play football, do you?' she asked him, although she knew football wasn't his bag. She wanted to keep him talking, to listen to his voice. 'Do you live in Lewes?'

'Up the town, Western Road.' Budgie appeared to bow his shoulders, almost to shrink when he said, 'I live with my father, and older brother.'

Bea noted his expression and body language as he mentioned his father, his reluctance to keep eye contact. She decided he was a person full of frustration; at some odds with his family. There was something else. A sadness that meant his face carried no danger of laughter lines. Both continued to fuss around with clothes and books.

Searching for a new topic to keep the conversation going, Bea said, 'You've got big exams coming up.'

'Mmm,' he muttered, with no trace of enthusiasm.

Bea thought, *he's uncertain about the now, uncertain about his future.* As they both went to class, she realised she'd enjoyed finding out a little about Budgie and he seemed to have enjoyed the chat too, although there was no smile on his face, not even when he said, 'Nice talking, see you round,' as he walked off.

19

That Sunday Bea had a training session to see how she fared with the older girls, who'd all welcomed her warmly. She knew she did well, with some good touches. They coached her to practice running off the ball into space. As soon as she'd showered and after a quick bite to eat, she made her way to Alana's. Jack had phoned earlier to say, 'Give her my love and tell her I hope to see her soon.'

Bea knocked on the front door and waited. She'd lost the discomfort and some of the guilt she carried about their last meeting, the awful episode when she'd let her friend down. Now she just had to embrace Alana, say sorry, and find out all that had happened to her. Bea wanted to be careful about reporting the positive things that were happening for her. As she waited she slipped the medal that she'd pressed tightly into her palm back into her pocket, making sure it was secure by placing her hand over her jeans to feel the thin contour.

'Come in, Bea,' said Mrs Lane. Bea followed Alana's mum into the family living room. 'Are things okay with you?'

'Yes, thanks.' Bea swiftly scanned the room and looked through to the conservatory half expecting to see a figure in a chair with a blanket across her knees.

'She's in her room,' smiled Mrs Lane. 'You can go up. Can I get you something?'

'No, I'm good, thanks,' said Bea, and turned to climb the stairs.

'Bea. You *will* remember what I said?'

Bea gave a weak smile and nodded.

Alana's door was open. Bea could see her in bed staring at a device, bony fingers at the end of painfully thin arms, working at a game. Alana looked up when, in the same movement, Bea tapped the door and tiptoed in. A smile welcomed her, reminding Bea in an instant of another Alana. She'd anticipated sunken cheeks, but not the difference to Alana's lovely hair. It was still long, but thinned and had lost its gorgeous lustre. Fortunately, for both patient and visitor, as they hugged their strong bond overtook any self-consciousness, as natural as yin to yang.

'Hello you,' said both together, and laughed. Where to begin?

'You first,' said Bea.

Alana recounted all the experiences over the weeks that had brought her ordinary life to an abrupt halt. She told of the mystery disease that had chosen to attack her, the grip it took on her body, the wonderful people who had helped sustain her when she was so tired and felt she wanted to die. She told Bea about the consultant who only last week had finally ruled out leukaemia.

Bea listened, taking a tissue from a box beside the bed.

'It's okay. It's just one of those things that happen, with no warning, no reason,' Alana said, smiling again.

'But—'

'Honestly, I mean this, I didn't even get to consider the *why me* bit. It just, like, never occurred to me.'

'So, what is it, Lan, what's happening?'

'They finally figured out that I've got what they call pernicious anaemia; I had to Google it. If it's caught in time, and it has been, I should make a good recovery, and that includes the hair,' she said twirling a tortuously thin strand in her fingers. "I just take like shitloads of vitamins. And I get to have a goth face without the make-up, so that's great!'

'I can't believe this is happening. And I haven't brought you anything either, except love from me, and Jack too.'

'Well, I won't be passing to you or sending over any crosses, at least for a while, if you can live with that. I can't tell you all at once, Bea. I've got some real sad stories from the hospital. Naturally they put me in the kid's ward, which was a bit of an indignity, but initially I was too ill to care. But later, as the days turned into weeks, I just looked about me and it was heart-breaking.

'At least I'd had a bit of a life, but the little ones…it was as if I could handle sick adults, in my head I mean, but kids can't rationalise things the same, why they feel so shit, what's happening and stuff. At least that's what I thought, even though on good days, when they felt better for a while, they were so happy. The second worst bit was waiting, not so much boredom but, like, what the hell's wrong here? Am I coming through this? And you can't sleep at night, that's when most of the activity seemed to happen. I'll tell you some more after. So, now you, what's been happening?'

Despite her intentions to be guarded it felt natural to tell Alana all her news. Bea started with school stories then summarised her football news. She'd helped Lewes reach the Under16 Girls Sussex Challenge Cup quarter-finals, she'd been scouted, the offer from Brighton, followed by the Girl's Development Pathway at Lewes. She talked about her parents,

Dad having to face court, and possibly wanting them to move to Brighton. Then the night out and how she enjoyed her first taste of alcohol. It all tumbled out of her and Alana got out of breath laughing at Tisha being sick at the end of the night.

Bea even told her about her meeting with Budgie, how she thought he was interesting, and did Alana know anything about him? Quite carried away, without really thinking, Bea poured out the story of the *magic medal*. 'Gramps took such care, cutting and sewing the boot. It was something about the way he looked at me. He really meant it.' She stopped short of telling Alana the medal was in her pocket.

Thankfully, Alana didn't scoff. She said, 'So, what difference has it made? You make it sound a bit creepy.'

'Well, he said, *Belief, is like faith. It makes unexpected things happen. Be patient, continue to work hard, Believe.* And, I don't know, something seems to have happened to me. Something feels like…different…in me. Ever since, I can't stop scoring goals, but more than that, I play really, really good every game.'

'No change there then, girl.'

'No. There is. I've never felt anything like it before. It's as if I can't fail. Whenever I get the ball I feel like I can't go wrong. It's like destiny. I know I'm gonna make it if, like, that's what I want. It…it's uncanny.'

'Bea, that's incredible.'

'And, I have to sleep with it under my pillow every night until match day.'

'Now this is getting a bit much. You're saying—'

'Look, I know how it sounds, Lan. You mustn't breathe a word. I'd just die if—'

'It's okay, really, but I'm coming along to see you play as soon as I can. Then I'll know. I'll know if there's a difference. I'll see it.'

150

An hour passed in a flash, and gradually Alana became less animated. It was nearly time to go. She told Bea her parents were talking of arranging for a tutor to come in twice a week, in addition to stuff her mum was going to get from school. Alana wasn't sure the thought inspired her. In answer to Bea's question, she said she hadn't been able to think much about Jack, what he meant to her, what if anything, she might mean to him. She knew her parents weren't keen on a lot of different visitors, but Bea should tell people she'd return their texts now she was starting to feel a bit better. The girls embraced. 'Give my love to Mrs Winks; not!' Alana joked.

It was only after she'd said goodbye to Mrs Lane and left the house that Bea realised she hadn't said *sorry*. But maybe that didn't matter – that space between them had been filled.

Bea phoned her mum to say she'd call in with Gramps for a while, As usual, she rapped on the door before letting herself in. Only her dad was in the living room, stretched in an easy chair with his legs straight out and feet on a stool. His hands, cut and bruised, were resting in his lap. Bea gasped at the sight. Brian's eyes were open, but closed. His nose looked to be almost at a right-angle to his face, and one of his eyebrows appeared to have disappeared. An indescribable feeling arose in her that made her want to laugh and cry at the same time.

'I thought I heard you,' said Gramps, popping his head round the door. 'How are you, my darling?'

Bea gave Gramps a peck on his cheek and sat opposite Brian, in silence, waiting.

'Bike,' said Brian at last.

Gramps joined them and, because no one spoke at first, Bea's suspicion was confirmed. In fact, the conversation was carried on between Bea and Gramps whilst Brian pretended to listen to the radio next to his ear. Eventually Bea turned to her father and asked what had really happened to him. The atmosphere in the room was awkward. Gramps rose to put the kettle on, but all Bea could get from her dad was, 'Things are settled now.'

Bea felt a mix of emotions looking at her father, exasperation not the least of them, in spite of his injuries. She went out to the kitchen to embrace Gramps, who merely offered her a peculiar expression, raising and lowering his brows, and with that she left.

More stuff to dwell on as she walked home. Bea wondered, not for the first time, whether Dad was a lost cause. He'd had his moment, like a shooting star that carried an aura but had burnt out and would never catch the eye ever again. *I'm a teenager looking out for her dad.* Bea was beginning to grasp Tisha's attitude toward him, and Mum's disappointment in a man who wouldn't grow up.

20

'We never used to see daffodils so early,' said Sandy. 'Let's cheer up, spring is in the air!'

'Spring gets earlier every year,' said Janis. 'I just wish he didn't have to go away so much.'

The pair had just seen Jack's dad, Sean, off again in his monster truck, heading for Dover and continental Europe. Petra was walking sedately with the sisters along the river bank.

'Why don't you have an affair?' laughed Sandy.

'You more like. What about Getgo? I saw the way he looked at you the other day on the touchline.'

'Don't be ridiculous! The man's too young,' she laughed. 'And it'd hardly be ethical, him in a romance with a parent. He'd get the sack and be struck off from whatever body rogue teachers get struck off from.'

'What are you going to do about Brian then?' Janis looked at her sister, silent in thought for a moment.

'He's landed in that hotel, he claims he's put his gambling behind him, and...well, he's not with anyone. And once he's finished those community service hours he got from the court, hopefully that's him done with the criminal justice system for good! I can't deny the change in him, Jan.

'I did wonder, when he arrived with another smartphone for Bea, and gave Tisha £250. But he swore on his father's life it was legitimate, and said he owed them. I'm glad Tisha's more...well, kindly toward him. It *has* made me think what we once meant to each other. I've only ever known Brian, and I'm not aware of anyone else ever seriously being in his life. Mind you, I wasn't following his life that closely for a lot of years.'

'What's he said to you?'

'I'm not sure. Me and the girls are alright as we are. You know that policeman Tisha saw a few times? They didn't hit it off. Thankfully she laughed when he told her he didn't feel they were right for each other. Bea phones to speak to her Gramps every day, making sure Brian's looking out for him, seeing he has all he needs. Major change for us is the last thing on my mind. We're happy as we are.'

At home, Bea greeted her mum, 'Hope you're hungry, tea's ready!'

'Oh, that's good, what is it?'

'Only macaroni cheese, but Tisha's baked a jam sponge.'

'Sounds ace,' said Sandy. 'I'll just get a quick wash.'

After Sandy had eaten she told the girls about her client, old Roger, having been taken to hospital and how fond she was of him. She asked Bea, 'Have you spoken to Gramps today?'

'I have,' said Bea. 'He's fine. He said Dad's looking after him, and been out shopping for them.'

Bea was less enthusiastic when the subject of her school project came up. She took herself off, put on her headphones, and lay back on her bed. When Tisha came to the door asking did she want some company, Bea answered, 'No, not really.'

She reached into her pocket for the *magic medal* and moved it between her fingers...*that's a medal waiting to be won*, Gramps had said. Bea still wasn't sure what that meant, just Gramps going on as he did sometimes. She thought to herself that Gramps' insights could still be quite profound, although he'd started to go on sometimes about little of any consequence. Immediately she felt bad for thinking that. She wouldn't know what she'd do if the old man wasn't in her life…if she lost him for some reason. She studied the medal, just making out the image of the panels and laces that illustrated an old-fashioned football. She slipped it under her pillow. Just then, she got a text from Budgie, **Sum of us r meeting 2morrow railway land by bridge…u no it?**

After their first conversation in school, Bea and Budgie had started acknowledging one another, saying 'Hi' and eventually they exchanged numbers. There was a sad something about him that intrigued her. One morning she learned from talk in school that his father had been sent to prison, so it was just him and his elder brother in the house. That afternoon Budgie had told her, 'They'll want to put me in foster care…over my dead body.'

Having decided to call Alana, Bea ignored his text for the moment.

'What's happening, Lan?' she said when Alana picked up.

Alana related the minutiae of her day with the home tutor. 'Some days I feel stronger than others. I haven't been out yet, but I'm the house walking-up-and-down-stairs champion.' They laughed, but Alana hesitated when Bea told her she was thinking of meeting up with Budgie tomorrow.

'What?' said Bea.

'What?'

'You've gone all silent on me.'

'No…nothing. It's just that I didn't think you'd have anything in common with him, except he's not bad looking.'

'Why, what d'you know about him?'

'We've never had anything to do with his lot, that's all. He's into boxing isn't he? And he doesn't say much. He's not a loudmouth like some of the ones he hangs with. Where are you going?'

'Don't know. I might not bother,' Bea said, trying to sound non-committal.

'Does Jack know?'

'No. Have you spoken to him?'

'Of course, we talk almost every day.'

Bea was glad she felt okay when Alana said that. The old feelings weren't there anymore.

Alana finished by telling Bea she wished she'd done a daily video *get well* diary on-line. 'Except that I look awful. I could wear a hat, or one of those cool scarf jobs the girls used to wear in the war, you know the ones.'

'It's a great idea. You're beautiful, Lan.'

'You too. Love you. Be careful.'

Bea's phone beeped with another text from Budgie, **Weather bril 2morrow meet rail land bridge at 11 c'mon.**

Bea stirred when she heard her mum leave for work at 6.30am. She turned over, contemplating going back to sleep, but the sun streaming in placed her on the edge of wakefulness, when imagination is brief but boundless. Her thoughts were jumbled and made no sense, until she heard herself mumble, 'I'm fucking fed up being sensible.'

Now she was alert and her consciousness transported her to the railway land, where she imagined she saw Budgie sitting, unsmiling. She sat bolt upright, drew up her knees and admired her golden arms wrapped around them. Outside was an early morning silence. No engine sounds, no seagull shrieks for once, nothing.

Bea got up and put on her dressing gown. No sound from Tisha. She went downstairs to make coffee, but stopped to look out of the living room window. Nothing was moving. In the kitchen she poured boiling water into a mug of instant coffee. She knew then that she'd meet Budgie. She texted him saying, C u later.

Since she lost weight Bea had been wearing Tisha's jeans. She wondered could she borrow her leather jacket, but decided against asking. Anyway, the day was unusually mild and the sky blue. She'd find a top, and wear her summer sandals. They were so shabby now, some would consider them chic. Bea had taught herself not to contend with the cool-trainer crowd. She couldn't compete if she wanted to. From the sofa she flicked through the channels, nothing but American sit-coms and food programmes, so she flicked until she found a radio channel, music that she kept down low. She went upstairs trying not to make a sound, and found a worn baggy jumper belonging to her mum. If it could speak it would say, *couldn't care less*. Perfect, she thought, and hauled it over her head. By 9 o'clock it was still too early but, as there was still no sign of Tisha, Bea decided to leave so that she wouldn't have to answer any questions. She could walk along the riverbank as far as she liked, and make her way back to the bridge whenever. She slung a cloth bag across her shoulders. In it was a bottle of water, her phone and a notebook. On top of her golden hair she'd donned a purple beret belonging to Tisha. She thought she looked cool. Hopefully, Budgie would think so, too. She touched her pocket feeling for the thin contour. There it was.

21

Bea tripped across the road, through the gap known only to dog walkers and joggers, and on to the earth path. She found herself in a different world, a wilderness both in and apart from the town, hidden in plain sight. Thoughts of football, family and friends were momentarily lost as she followed the river southwards listening to the birdsong. She dipped down an incline on the bank and looked into the water. The river was tidal and could alter from filmy brown to almost clear from day to day. Bea knew that the fish were often hard to spot, but once you saw one, there was another and another. She marvelled at the size of some of them, silver and brown going about their business near the edges of the bank. Occasionally, a runner jogged by. This morning the dog walkers were few. As she climbed back to the path she spied a shape far in the distance. It took a while to register whether the figure was walking in the same direction as she was, or moving toward her. By the time she decided it was approaching her she recognised who it was, Budgie, clearly lifting a can to his mouth. She was trying to think of what she would to say to him when, suddenly she was furious as she witnessed him tossing the empty can nonchalantly into the bank.

Bea quickened her pace. He saw her. His face broke into a rare smile, on then off as quickly as a blown light bulb. His brief smile was not returned. At a short distance Bea called, 'I can't believe you did that.'

Budgie looked puzzled, 'Did what?'

'I saw you toss that can into the bank.'

'What's your problem?' He removed a small but bulky backpack, put it at his feet, reached in and offered her a special brew. 'Here, relax,' he said.

'I won't relax,' she said angrily. 'Not until we go back and find that rubbish you just tossed into this countryside.'

Budgie looked startled and put the can back. 'Okay.'

The pair walked in silence to where Bea reckoned it should be. They found it easily enough.

'Well go on,' she said.

He looked between her and the can. Then he scrambled half way down the bank to lift it. Crushing it and stuffing it into his back-pack he climbed up, reaching out a hand, but Bea stood resolutely. When he got to the top, she said, 'Good,' and walked a few meters further to take a seat on a bench just off the path. Budgie sat beside her, opened a fresh can, which this time Bea accepted and opened one for himself. She was becoming used to him being a guy of few words.

Bea took a swig of the special brew, it was sour, unlike the cocktails she'd enjoyed with Tisha and the girls. This was her first taste of beer and she tried hard not to screw her face up.

She looked at him. 'Can you, like, not do that.'

'What?'

'You know what. Why did you?'

Budgie leant forward and stared at his feet, 'I dunno. Everything's shit.'

159

'If that's what you feel,' she replied. 'Only there's some stuff,' she went on, gesturing with a sweep of her arm, 'still worth respecting, that isn't shit.'

Budgie took another swig from his can. 'You look different. Nice.'

'You too,' she said. After a moment, she asked, 'How old are you?'

'Nearly seventeen…and you're fifteen.'

Bea took a long drink and offered a weak smile of her own. 'So you're sixteen. How many of these have you had?'

'Couple.'

'It's strong. I can feel it already.' Another moment's silence followed. 'I heard about your dad,' she said.

'Best place for him.'

Bea looked about her, taking in the space around them. 'D'you wanna talk about it?'

'Nah…some other time maybe.' He'd almost finished his can. His third of the morning if he hadn't been lying. 'The others'll be here in a bit.'

'Do I know any of them?'

'There's a couple from my class in school you'll know to see, two of my cousins, and a girlfriend of one of them.'

'Are your cousins from here?'

'They're coming up from Brighton.'

'Okay.'

Bea started to ask how he was getting on with some big exams his year would be sitting, but Budgie wasn't keen to talk about school. She asked about training at the boxing club. He gave another fleeting smile, more like a grimace, and raised his can.

'Your smile reminds me of the sun poking through clouds before it disappears again.'

He laughed for the first time, 'That's pretty good.'

'Have you quit training then?'

'Oh, I dunno. I really sort of want boxing sometimes, but other times I can't be bothered.'

'Mmm. I imagine thumping a punch-bag would be good therapy, especially if you're feeling everything's shit.'

He didn't answer. Bea wasn't enjoying the taste of the strong beer, although its effect reminded her of how much she enjoyed the buzz she felt on the cocktail night with Tisha.

He stood.

She felt a dubious excitement rising in her as they headed over to the bridge, beside which was the remains of an old wall, its place and purpose lost in history. Bea knew of it as a spot where people Budgie's age and older gathered to smoke dope and mess about. She'd always avoided it and was wary, determined to remain on her guard.

When Jack phoned, Alana told him that she'd never been as bored in her life.

'I'm writing a book,' he joked. 'How to stimulate boredom when you have nothing better to do.'

'Not funny, Jack.'

'I'd like to see you,' he said.

'You *can* see me, you are seeing me, this is me now with my lovely hair,' she laughed.

'I don't mean on a screen!'

'When I can, we'll take Petra to the Priory, just as soon as I re-emerge into the world. I keep on at mum, so it shouldn't be long now.'

'I'll bet you envy Bea out every day running. Even Tisha is going with her nowadays.'

'Well she's not running today. She's meeting up with that guy, Budgie…Jack, have you gone to sleep?'

'Oh my God, do tell me you're joking.'

'I'm not joking, why?'

'Budgie's father is Mathew Budgell and he's a nasty piece of work.'

'How do you know?'

'What I've picked up being nosey. Overheard conversations between my mum and Bea's. He's one of the ones involved with Bea's dad. Or, like, against Bea's dad I should say.'

The pair considered what Jack knew about Matt Budgell's history.

'What would Bea make of that?' said Alana.

'She has to know. Do you want to tell her?'

'Do you?'

'One of us should.'

'She's not gonna get serious about the guy.'

'Maybe, maybe not,' said Jack. 'Remember, her grandad took a beating as well. She ought to be told before anything does happen between them. Believe me, it'd change everything.'

'I'm against telling her until we actually know that…I mean we should wait until we're together and the conversation turns that way. Let Bea mention him first.'

'Okay, we'll do that. She'll phone us anyway. If you tell her first, let me know.'

Bea and Budgie reached the meeting spot located a little way from a clear-running stream that fed into the river. In a few short weeks, with the new growth of spring, the old wall they sat on would be totally secluded from walkers crossing the wooden bridge within voice distance. The path from the bridge took people in a semi-circle around the wall and on through the trees. Bea was thinking of ways she could coax Budgie's conversation, to hear the voice she liked so much. She was encouraged that she'd actually made him laugh, albeit briefly. How difficult could the task be? They sat for five minutes, Bea struggling on her second can, before they heard the others shouting and laughing. When they appeared Budgie offered a terse introduction. The guys ignored her, but the girl, Steph, smiled. Bea smiled back.

Steph presented a tall brown bottle. 'D'you want some cider, Bea?'

It was good that she used my name, thought Bea, feeling relaxed. The girls shared it, and Bea, feeling energised, passed the remainder of her can to Budgie.

'I can drink this better,' she said to Steph.

'Drink up then, I've got another bottle here.'

One of the guys started to roll a joint. Bea was feeling as she did on the night out in Brighton, but knew there was no way she was going to smoke. She was glad when Budgie refused it, too. Calum, the loudest of the newcomers, kept on at them.

'Go on try it, it's good stuff.'

'Not for me,' said Bea, 'I'll stick to cider, thanks.'

'Don't know what you're missing,' said Calum, persisting. 'Alcohol's worse for you.'

'There's a difference,' said Bea.

A debate began about alcohol and other drugs, with Bea insisting there was a difference, Calum insisting a drug is a drug, and that alcohol was definitely a drug.

'What's wrong with you?' he continued.

'Leave it,' said Budgie sharply.

Loudmouth immediately ran on to something else, hoping to cover his embarrassment at Budgie's intervention, but the message to him was clear. The other cousin, Danny, asked Budgie had he heard anything.

Budgie replied, 'A man and a woman were at the house yesterday.'

Bea turned to him, 'What about?'

'They were from the Education, I think, about the foster care business. My brother wouldn't let them in.'

'So, what are you going to do?'

'Avoid them,' he said.

Bea sensed this wasn't the time or place for this conversation and, anyway, the rest of the group had started laughing wildly, still passing the joint around. She began to feel a bit uncomfortable and suggested to Budgie that they go for a walk. What she meant was she wanted an end to the gathering, for *her* at least. Budgie watched her stand and without saying anything, agreed.

They walked close. He put a tentative arm around her. Just long enough to say, 'Sorry,' before it withdrew. But it was a start.

'Tell me about your lot,' he said, as the two of them made tracks back along the way they came, 'your family.'

Bea saw this as a way to learn more about him. She told him about Mum and Tisha first, then Dad, and finally Gramps, but only the barest details.

She learned from him about his mother leaving home because of violence at the hands of his father. His mother had what he termed, 'Like, too many problems of her own and moved around a lot.

'It'd be impossible for me to live with her. My father's been in trouble with the police as long as I can remember. I've been in foster care a few times, when I was a kid.'

Bea thought she could listen to his voice all day, but wished it was reciting poetry, or something. Instead, the background he described revealed so much about his silences, the unhappiness burning through him.

'I'm glad you agreed to meet me today. They weren't a good idea, sorry about that,' he said pointing a thumb over his shoulder.

'You don't have to apologise again.'

'They said they were coming over, so I said I'd see them. I don't know why I thought it'd be a good idea to include you. They're not the crowd for you.'

'Steph seemed alright. You don't do drugs, do you?'

'Nah. My brother, Jamie, stinks the place out smoking. I've tried stuff. I don't like it.'

Bea said, 'I can't believe this, but I don't know your real name.'

'It's Steve.' He smiled, and the light stayed on a bit longer. 'Steve Budgell.'

22

That evening Bea was lying on her bed listening to music, going over the day's events when Budgie phoned.

'Hi, I was just wondering, er...can we meet up again tomorrow? I was thinking I'd like to talk some things through with you.'

'Cool. Are you at home now?'

'I'm home, yeah, if you could call it home. It's just with things happening...I feel I could talk to you about stuff.'

'Do you wanna go for a walk? We could go up Chapel Hill, and on to the Downs.'

'Great. Can we say Cliffe Bridge? Early as poss for me.'

'Catch you there at nine if you want?' Bea said and waited.

'I enjoyed today,' Budgie said at last. 'See you tomorrow.'

Bea was concerned that he sounded anxious, and knew there must have been a lot of thought before he made the call. It had probably been difficult for him to say he'd enjoyed today. In the short time she'd spent in his company she believed there was more to Budgie than the hard-headed tough guy he presented. For the first time in her life, Bea checked on her phone for tomorrow's weather. It said continuing mild and dry. She smiled to herself. Later, as she tried to sleep, she realised that was the first day she hadn't spoken to either Jack or Alana, or both. She turned over on her front and slipped her hand under her pillow, wishing now that she'd never mentioned anything about the medal to Alana. Why had she? It should've been just me and you Gramps. She fell fast asleep.

In her dream, she stood in Southover Grange Gardens. She saw Gramps. It was as if they were in heaven together, surrounded by a budding spring garden. It was warm and the sun was out. She felt a resounding and overwhelming compassion watching the old man limping along the path from a distance, turning his head this way and that to spot her. She remembered him as he had been, running after a football in the park with her and Tisha. She waved, walking toward him.

'Ah, my darling,' said the old man.

'What have you been doing with yourself, Gramps?'

'Same as always, radio, my crosswords, bit of reading, telly. Time for me isn't pedestrian like it is for you young people, but I haven't half missed you all the same.'

'Why? I haven't been anywhere.'

Gramps laughed. 'Haven't you? I thought you had.'

'Gramps.'

In her dream, once more she regretted telling Alana about her medal, not because she couldn't trust her, but she felt that, somehow, she'd betrayed Gramps.

Bea was up early as usual. She didn't shower, but washed her face, fixed and tied up her hair. She pulled on another pair of jeans Tisha had given her, and placed her medal carefully in the pocket. Despite the forecast, there was a chill in the morning air. She had on her vest, a long-sleeved tee-shirt, and placed her old tracksuit top on. When she checked in the mirror it told her again that it was too small and looked ridiculous. Should she freeze for a bit and trust to the walking, or... In a drawer she found an ideal chunky sweater with long sleeves and a high midriff that she could peel off and stuff in her cloth bag. Downstairs she went for toast as opposed to cereal, with a half mug of coffee. She didn't want to fill up because they could be hours on the Downs.

Just before she set off, Alana phoned. 'Bea, I've got some great news.'

'Brilliant, what is it?'

'I've worn mum down, so I'm allowed to meet Jack to go to the Priory with him and Petra.'

'Great, Lan – when?'

'This afternoon. I had to promise faithfully to be sensible and, naturally, knowing me I'll be just that,' she laughed. 'Will you call over for me?'

Alana was surprised to hear the hesitancy in Bea's voice.

'What time were you thinking? It's just I'm going for a walk with Budgie in a bit, so it sort of depends what's going down after.'

Alana was careful not to hesitate like her friend and said, 'Oh, you're seeing Budgie again. Okay, you'll have to tell us about it. I'll probably leave here about two and stroll over to Jack's.'

'I'll text you guys, anyway. See ya later!'

Even though she got to the bridge before 9am, Budgie was already waiting, sitting on a bench overlooking the river.

'Hi.'

'Hi. Thanks for coming,' he said, getting up to give her a quick hug, which pleased her.

'Shall we crack on?' she said, with a nod of her head. 'It's easier to talk and walk I think. Don't you?'

Budgie delivered one of his on-off smiles that Bea was certain he must have practised in a mirror. He said nothing while they walked toward the end of the street, until he stopped to buy them coffees to go. Bea noted they cost him a fiver. It was the route she and Alana had taken only a few months back, when she imagined she'd developed a crush on her.

When they reached the junction with South Street she laughed as she recalled what had happened there before. 'So, where were you when Alana twisted that idiot's nose?'

'Right over there,' he said, nodding toward a seat outside the old church.

'A lot's happened since then.'

'To me,' he said.

'And to me.'

They stopped and sipped their drinks.

'Here's the long haul,' said Bea. 'Are you up for it?'

'After you,' said Budgie, and the pair set off on the steep climb to the top, on to the Downs overlooking the town.

His conversation skills hadn't transformed overnight and he said little on their way up. But that was comfortable because breath was demanded even for the fittest to make it up safely, practically in one go. And they had all day.

They stopped only to finish their coffees and take in the sprawling arena of towns, villages and countryside below. Eventually at the summit, Bea said, 'Let's head this way.' She set a slow pace, a pace ideal for talking, and waited for him to start.

'We've got another week of this before school,' she said, trying to encourage him.

'Not for me,' said Budgie.

'Tell me.'

'I can't go back, can I? I couldn't even if I wanted to. Social services for a start, and you heard about the break-in?'

Bea shook her head.

'Someone broke into one of the craft studios at the school. They're always after someone to blame and guess who fitted the bill?'

'What are you going to do?'

'I don't know. The stupid system didn't join up until they looked for my so-called parent or guardian over it. By that stage he'd already been inside for weeks. They've called at the house a couple of times. The last time, Jamie told them to fuck-off. Now I can't go back to school....I'm not sure what to do.'

Bea felt as if Budgie was looking for an opinion from her, but she wasn't sure whether she was qualified to offer advice.

'How old is your brother?'

'Eighteen, but he's a prick, like our dad.'

'Is there no one who can look out for you? Who does all your stuff? You need to shop, cook, eat, wash clothes.'

'I look out for myself.'

Bea quickly calculated how tough that must be, and, because of it, she felt something close to admiration for him. 'What about money?' she asked.

Budgie's head went down, and Bea noticed the familiar slump of the shoulders. 'Money isn't usually a problem,' he said. 'Dad keeps money in the house.'

'But your dad's—'

'You wouldn't understand that side of things, Bea...money. He'll be out in a few weeks anyway.'

'What then?'

They walked on, batting away the spring insects that started to annoy them. After a while, Budgie said, 'I need to get away,

I can't live with them any longer. I mean I don't want to live with them.'

'Does he hit you?'

'It's not that, no. Bad stuff is hatched in that house. You want to hear them talking. No, on second thoughts, you don't.'

'Who?'

'Dad, and his mates.'

'Do you want to know what I think?' said Bea slowly.

Budgie stopped and looked at her. 'Yes.'

'You might not like this, but I think you must go to social services, or whoever it is, and, like, give yourself up.'

She appreciated it when Budgie didn't react badly to what she said. She could see he was thoughtful, and that was positive.

'If what you just told me is only half true, Budgie, you should try to get settled somewhere...with someone. You're supposed to sit exams soon, aren't you?'

He gave a scornful little laugh. 'No chance there. I'm not clever in that way. Homework was never my strong point, y'know. I thought I might make a living through boxing someday.'

'Budgie, that's not on for ages. Even I know that takes dedication, boxing for years for no money. No, you'll have to think of something else.'

'There's an uncle of mine, but he lives in Hastings. He's never had anything to do with Dad. He's my mother's brother. An electrician, but what would he take me on for? Maybe I could try for a skill like that.'

It was positive to hear Budgie talk that way, but he needed a base. Bea was sure he could thrive with stability in his life. No one need be a clone of their parents, she thought. No one should be labelled a lost cause unless they proved otherwise by their actions.

The sun rose and the morning chill burned off. The green of the Downs shone and Bea, her jumper now in her bag, felt the gentle wind reach out to her. They walked and talked and then walked in silence. She felt...comfortable, she thought.

On the walk back Budgie asked her more about her family. He was interested and said that she hadn't given much away yesterday. He listened carefully when she told him the *Windrush* tale, then her parent's history as she understood it, the way they had met in school.

'It all sounds a bit corny,' she laughed.

'It's cool, except they had to split up.'

'Yeah, I guess. Look, what are you doing later?'

'We could go and get something to eat if you like, on me. We could even go in somewhere.' He hesitated. 'I...I've got money.'

'We won't go in anywhere,' said Bea. 'We'll get something and eat it over by the river.'

'Great.'

When they reached the bottom of the hill Budgie wanted to go to the chip shop, but Bea persuaded him to follow her.

'This is far better for us, for me, anyway,' she said leading him to a healthy sandwich shop.

Coming back out on to the street she said, 'Thank you for my lunch.'

Budgie walked towards the river, looking at what he called, a brown bread sparrow sandwich. 'Don't mention it. *Really,*' he said making a joke of the last word. Another smile, on for longer than off this time.

They found a bench to sit and eat the sandwiches. Budgie had bought more coffee too. They listened to the rush of the river on its way out with the tide, mixed with shrieking birds squabbling on the banks.

'I'd like you to come over with me and meet Alana in the Priory later. It's her first day of freedom, first time out since she's been home. You know my cousin, Jack, everyone knows Jack. They'll be walking his dog over there.'

'I wouldn't mind. You know I'm not doing anything.'

Bea tried not to stare up at him, but she noted how good-looking he was, the kindness in his face when he laughed again. As they ate, she took up her family story with Gramps. When she told him what she loved about her Grandad, and how she cared for him so much, Budgie said he'd never known either of his grandfathers. She got to the bit about finding Gramps on his kitchen floor, slowly describing the state she found him in, and Budgie grew completely silent. At first Bea didn't notice, but when she stopped talking she sensed that something about the day had changed.

'We could walk over to the Priory now, and wait for them to show. I'll text Alana.'

'Wait,' said Budgie. Bea waited. 'I'm not sure I can go with you after all.'

'Oh,' she said, 'I thought —'

'I know, but there *is* something I need to do. I just remembered.'

'Okay…sure, that's a shame. I thought it'd be good to—'

'Don't get me wrong, Bea. I'd like to come with you, but…it's something I promised I'd help Jamie with. It's a drag for me y'know. I might have to go to Brighton with him. Maybe we can meet tomorrow, or sometime?'

'I'm playing in the morning,' said Bea, disappointed that he had changed his mind, 'but, yeah text me.'

'I will,' said Budgie.

'Be careful,' she called, 'and think about what I said.'

'I will definitely,' he said getting to his feet. 'I'm sorry, Bea. Really.' This time his last word was not said as a joke.

She watched him stride off and felt a little dejected. The day had been going great. She didn't know what had gone wrong. Or maybe he did have to help his brother.

Bea traipsed back through the town and despite it being Alana's first day out she decided to not go to the Priory. This would be Jack and Alana's first meeting alone. Let them be alone. Instead she got home, went to her bedroom, put on some music and mulled over Budgie and his troubles.

23

Sunday morning, Bea was up for an early breakfast. The match was an 11am kick-off, plenty of time to digest a boiled egg, multiple slices of buttered toast, and mugs of tea. She was determined to put Budgie into the mental compartments she kept, filed *not for this moment*. The girls were meeting outside the Pan at 10 for a coach to take them to Newhaven. Sandy and Tisha were still flapping about in their dressing gowns when Bea ran upstairs to complete her ritual. She took the medal from under her pillow. She slid it into the pocket cut into her boot, raised the boot, kissed it, and said, *'Believe'*. She placed the boots into her bag. The bedroom, in private, was absolutely the right place to perform this, not in the dressing room with her teammates looking on. She supposed it might be okay because lots of the girls, in fact most of them, had their own personal little rituals before a game – one always had to put her socks and boots on each leg separately, finish one side before the other; one insisted she had to pull her shorts on last of all; one always had to do ten push-ups and be last player out – but hers was a more personal, meditative affair. She didn't want to have to explain the whole thing.

Bea was glad Alana never mentioned the medal again, and was sworn to secrecy. This was still a thing between her and Gramps.

'I'm off,' she called, sticking her head through the living room door. Mum and Tisha, sitting in the kitchen over their coffee, shouted back, 'Good luck, score a *bagshotful*.' Bea filled her lungs with air as she hit the street. Although it was cloudy and dull she felt alive, fortified by the regular training routines undertaken over many months. Excitement kicked in approaching the Pan where she saw a group already there chatting noisily, just about outdone by the cawing of an on looking family of rooks.

'That's gotta be a good omen,' Bea thought.

When the girls spotted her everyone shouted their welcomes and hellos. There was genuine warmth and pleasure at her arrival. It made Bea feel really special. The thought that she was good enough to be in the team, let alone be scoring and playing so well as to be called their 'star player' by a report on the local news website, humbled and thrilled her. The recognition she remembered hadn't always been there, but now it added to her confidence.

Getgo arrived in his car, parked up and joined the group, rubbing his hands. 'Everyone fit?' They all shouted, '*Yay*,' as he saw them on to the vehicle. In twenty-five minutes they reached Newhaven Academy, but before they trooped off he stood at the front with a sober expression.

He waited for the hubbub to die down and for their attention to be focussed on him. 'I think…' he said, drawing out the pause until they were all looking as concerned as him. 'We're gonna give that lot a serious stuffin' today.' Another loud cheer went up.

The girls made for the Far Field pitch where some of the opposition were already knocking a ball about. *Getgo* took the team through the usual reaching and stretching routines and before long the teams were lined up with Bea waiting impatiently for the ref to blow for kick-off.

The first half was played out mostly in the middle of the park. A midfield battle-royal with only a couple of half-chances, one at either end. The one that fell to her, Bea felt she should have buried, but for some reason she chose to dwell too long on the ball, only to shoot wide from a few yards out. By the change around the game was still 0-0.

'Girls we're not creating enough chances,' said *Getgo* at the break. 'Our defence is good, well done, but we need more energy in midfield. Move the ball quicker.' Mindful to balance it out, he added, 'Up front as well. You're not linking the way your brilliant coach has drilled you!' The girls laughed politely.

As they took to the field for the second half, he said to Bea, 'I know you won't mind me saying, Bea, or I wouldn't say it, but have you got lead in your boots today?' Bea just nodded, grimaced, and thought to herself, *No, but I could tell you what I have got.* His comment was the spur she needed.

Five minutes into the second half and she dropped back, collecting the ball on half way, turning neatly, side-slipping an opposition midfielder left wallowing in her wake. A couple of touches to sort her feet out and then Bea accelerated down the wing like lightning. She danced inside another tackle, stepped over, shimmied right but went left and with great close control arrowed down the middle of the pitch in a straight line to shoot at the advancing 'keeper. Fair play, the keeper made herself big, stayed up until the last moment and just managed to get a hand on the shot, parrying it up and to the side where it dropped neatly at the foot of Bea's fellow forward, the Lewes No.10, who put her head down, took her time and side footed the ball into the open net. Bea rushed to congratulate her teammate.

'Easy as Bea, all your good work that made it!'

Over the course of the half Bea pictured the magic in her right boot urging her on. She believed in it and the effect still startled her. She knew she'd played average in the first half, but kept the image of the medal in her mind throughout the second. Even when Academy equalised from a headed corner, on the hour mark, Bea *knew* she would score before the final whistle. Not felt it. Not imagined it. *Knew* it.

With ten minutes to go, as low grey clouds scudded across the sky and the wind picked-up, swirling round the pitch, a loose ball from the left dropped in her path. Bea took it on her instep and shifted it to her left foot. A quick knock forward, then another step over and the defender made the mistake of watching Bea and not the ball. Bea feinted to go one way, allowed the ball to roll, pushed off on her left and switched right. The defender tried to turn and fell over her own feet. Bea didn't dwell on how the poor girl looked foolish. Instead, she looked up, ran another few paces, and got herself a clear sight on goal. The keeper was shifting sideways, covering the near post. Again, Bea heard Gramps telling her to, '*Hit it as hard as you can at an angle across the goalkeeper.*' Her boot struck the ball and she watched it drill into the far corner of the net. Unusually for her, Bea celebrated with clenched fists and a scream of, '*Yeeessss!*' It was as if life's recent ordeals were wiped in a moment, like an accelerated spring message to the sleeping earth, *Awake!*

Ideally, Bea would have preferred to sit to contemplate on her own on the bus home, but there was a balance to be struck. She was careful to join in the loud celebrations and be one of the girls, singing along with the others toward the back of the bus, '*We are, we are, we are the girls,*' before silently slipping away nearer the front, unnoticed by the jubilant fray. There'll be a hot shower and a roast dinner waiting, she thought. And then she thought about Budgie.

When Bea walked in, Tisha said, 'You won 2-1 and scored the winner'.

'How do *you* know?' said Bea.

'Your dad was watching you,' said Sandy. 'He's just left.'

'Ahh, I didn't see him, why didn't he say? He could've come over to us at the end.'

'You know your dad, he does strange things sometimes.'

'Most of the time,' said Tisha, but with a laugh.

'What did he want?'

Sandy said, 'He only dropped in for a quick chat about Gramps, and said to tell you, you were great in the second-half.'

'Well, what about Gramps? What did he say?'

'Gramps is okay, he couldn't stay because he's making dinner for them.'

'Just okay?'

'Yes Bea,' said Sandy, abruptly. 'He asked if you're going over this afternoon.'

'I might. I'm not sure, yet,' said Bea, running upstairs to the shower.

'Dinner's in twenty minutes,' Sandy called after her.

Bea took her boot from her bag and, with the tweezers Tisha had given her, eased the medal out. She smiled and placed it back under her pillow. The shower was roasting. She soaped all over and let the water soak into her. It felt good. Bea had been reading the latest advice on how beneficial it was to finish a shower with cold water, only a few seconds at first, but building up until being able to tolerate the cold for the last few minutes. She'd smashed lots of things in the previous months, but thought, *stuff that, I'll just stick with the deep breathing for now!*

After Sunday dinner there was no word from Budgie. Bea checked with Alana. She'd had a second Petra-walk that morning with Jack, but now she said she was bored again and asked Bea to drop by. Bea decided she would call on Gramps, so Alana invited her to stop on the way back to have tea.

Bea chose to walk through Southover Grange Gardens on her way. The low sky of the morning had relaxed and retreated to reveal a bright spring warmth. No sooner was she down the sloping pathway than the resident squirrel family was upon her, one actually racing up her thigh to stare her out. As much as she longed to, Bea was slightly concerned about touching the nosey creature lest it bite her, but it was away again in a second like quicksilver. She admired the beds of wildflowers in the making, bursting to greet the warmth. Lightweight now, awaiting the ardent attentions of the summer insects the world relies on. *This could easily get to be my best time of the year after all*, she said to herself.

By late afternoon when she arrived at Gramps' she'd already had an energetic day. There was no sign of Gramps in the living room when she walked in. Bea went through to the kitchen where Brian was rinsing suds off plates and placing them to one side.

'That's what I like to see,' she said. 'Where's Gramps?'

His hands wet, Brian hugged her loosely. 'Hey honey, he's gone for a lie down. I don't like to see him dozing in the chair after his meal, and he was happy to go.'

'That's good, Dad. How do you think he's coming on?'

'At his check-up the other day the doctor had no particular advice other than not to overdo things, and if he felt sleepy then sleep! He's a fighter and, thing is…he's not as able as he was, but that's understandable.'

'Mmm,' said Bea thoughtfully. 'Anyway, where were you watching this morning? Why didn't you come over?'

'Oh, I just thought I'd let you play your game, and I must say I was impressed. You've really come on. You perform like a natural striker.' Brian returned to his dishes.

Bea didn't offer to help dry, instead she went and sat in the chair facing the trophy cabinet. With no forethought, something gestating since yesterday came to mind. She leaned sideways and looked through to her dad, calling out casually, 'Do you know anyone named Budgell?'

Brian froze. He couldn't speak for a minute. 'What did you say?' he called back.

'I said do you know a man called Budgell?'

She watched her dad tense and heard the same in his voice. 'Why do you ask?' he said.

'I know his son from school. He's a friend of mine.'

Brian came to stand in the kitchen doorway with his arms straight at his sides and a look in his eyes that frightened Bea.

'What is it, Dad?' she said nervously.

'I'm asking you…I'm telling you to have nothing to do with that family.'

Bea sat, unable to speak.

Her dad left the room. He was only gone a few minutes before returning. The tension in the room was almost visible.

Bea wanted to challenge the order he'd given her but her courage failed her. In a flash she remembered her walk with Budgie and the range of feelings that had been stirred in her whilst listening to him speak about his family. She had caught sight of a vulnerability about him, a gentle quality, and his tough life had drawn from her a sort of admiration. Was she about to learn something that would wipe all that away? She couldn't carry this on just now. She was confused and had never seen Dad look like he did. Bea stood up, as her dad sat down frowning. She was too scared to embrace him.

'I promised to call at Alana's for tea,' she said sullenly.

Her dad sat forward. He looked up briefly, then back at the floor.

She turned to go, saying, 'Tell Gramps I'll see him soon.'

To her ears, her dad sounded almost breathless when he spoke. 'Remember what I said.'

'We can speak again,' she called defiantly, not knowing what to think.

After she left, Brian sat and wept. He'd gambled heavily that week, and lost.

Alana answered the door. They went through for Bea to say 'Hello' to Mrs Lane, then took coffees upstairs. Sandwiches were promised in a bit. Alana's room looked more inviting than ever. A kaleidoscopic *Frida Kahlo* had appeared on one of the walls and smaller cut-outs of the artist and her work were dotted about.

Alana looked at Bea. 'Okay, what's happened?' Bea shook her head. She carried her coffee carefully and sat in the one easy chair in Alana's room. 'Is it Budgie?'

'What?'

'Have you spoken to Jack about him?'

'No, I haven't spoken to Jack. What's he got to do with Budgie?'

'Okay, you haven't spoken to Jack, but something's happened.'

'Can we start again?' protested Bea. 'I wish someone would tell me what the fuck is going down.'

'Right,' said Alana. 'Obviously something's happened to upset you before you arrived. What is it?'

'I've come from Gramps' place but only saw my Dad, and he was—'

'Where's your Gramps?'

'That's not the point! He was in bed. I asked Dad did he know anyone called Budgell, and he totally freaked. Practically told me I was to have nothing to do with the Budgell family, and said no more. That was it...but the look on his face, it scared me. Now where does Jack come in?'

'Bea, Jack knows something about the Budgells, but you'll have to ask him.'

'I don't believe this.'

Mrs Lane opened the door carrying a plate of sandwiches and cake. 'Lots of language going on, girls,' she said. 'What are you two so heated about?'

'It's nothing, Mum.'

Mrs Lane looked at Bea. 'If anyone needs me I'm downstairs,' she said, and closed the door.

'So, you and Jack have been discussing the Budgells, or Budgie, and saying nothing to me. What do you know, Lan?'

Alana said, 'Let's have a sandwich.'

24

On her way home Bea phoned Jack, demanding he tell her all he knew about the Budgell family.

'Don't blame Alana,' said Jack, 'I only told her what I'd heard after she said you were meeting up with Budgie. We agreed it was best if we waited for you to tell us about Budgie before one of us said anything. Alana was getting her information second hand from me, so—'

'You're becoming quite the little private detective aren't you, Jack?' Bea said. The anger in her voice was unmistakable.

'Come on, Bea. Our mums meet here more often than at your place, otherwise it would be you picking up on stuff, instead of me.'

'So, tell me what you know.'

'Only that the first time I heard the name Budgell mentioned was after that awful attack on your Gramps; when he was in hospital, and your mum was really upset.'

Bea was beginning to put it together now and her feelings towards Budgie were unravelling. She was almost home but couldn't wait any longer. There was all evening left for her to quiz her mother. She stopped and phoned Budgie but he didn't pick up. She waited, and called again. Still he didn't answer. Bea texted him that she wanted to speak to him. Urgently.

When she reached home, her mum had a meal on her lap, watching the news. She looked up, 'Hi love, have you eaten?'

'Yes, at Alana's. There's something I have to talk to you about when you're finished. I'm going upstairs.'

Ten minutes later her mum called up, 'I'm ready.' There was no response. Sandy climbed the stairs. She could see through the open bedroom door. Bea was writing something in a notebook.

'Hi, I'm all yours,' said Sandy.

'Will you sit down, Mum? This is serious.'

Sandy looked apprehensive, but sat on the bed and waited.

'Mum, do you know someone called Budgell?'

'Budgell,' Sandy repeated with a hint of alarm in her voice.

'Yes. Do you know someone called that?'

Her mum paused momentarily, took a breath and said, 'Yes, I know of a man, Budgell. He lives local.'

'I was talking to Dad at Gramps' earlier on. Gramps was having a lie down. I told Dad I knew this man's son, told him that he was a friend of mine. I've never seen such an expression on his face. He practically ordered me never to see Budgie…that's my friend, Steve Budgell, again. I didn't challenge Dad because, well, he sort of scared me. Who does he think he is talking to me like that? And what's this about?'

'He's your father, Bea, although,' Sandy said deliberately, 'there was no excuse for his reaction to scare you. I understand why it might, though. You see, Budgell is…was, one of the ones Dad was involved with.' She looked intently at Bea. 'If you're telling me that you're friends with his son, I'm worried, too.'

In spite of all she'd learned, and was still learning, Bea heard herself saying, 'Well you needn't be. Budgie's not like that. He's not like the rest of them. He doesn't even like his father, he told me.'

'How well do you know this…Budgie? What made you mention him to your father?'

'I know him from school. We've been for a walk a couple of times. He's unhappy. He told me a lot about his father and his brother, and he's not, like, one of them. I mentioned him because of things he'd told me about his father. I thought Dad might know of him.'

Sandy let Bea carry on, at the same time considering how to respond. At last she said, 'No one has been found by police, yet…for the attack on Gramps. Until they have we can't be certain, but—'

'Are you saying..? What *are* you saying?'

'I'm saying, Bea, that nothing's been proved against that man. Police are still investigating, also,' Sandy said, holding her hand up to stop Bea from interrupting, 'you never mentioned you had a new friend, but you really do need to think carefully before you get fond of this boy.'

Bea was incensed Budgie hadn't responded to her message. Despite that she was confused whether she wanted to see him, or even whether she wanted to hear him out. That's why he went quiet when I mentioned Gramps, she thought. That's why he didn't pick up. That's why he didn't even respond when I said I needed to see him. He knows something. The coward!

Though she was exhausted, Bea slept fitfully that night. In her nonsensical dream, she was sitting in a wheelchair watching Gramps arguing with Budgie. Gramps was accusing Budgie, telling him everything was all his fault; he was pointing at her, saying, 'Look at her.' Budgie was crying. Then Bea lifted out of

186

the wheelchair, desperate to get away from the scene. She found she could fly, simply by willing it. Her arms were across her chest, her legs pedalling like on a bicycle, but it was taking a huge effort to maintain height. Although she travelled across the town, in spite of massive physical effort she couldn't rise as high as she needed to avoid people staring and pointing at her. There was a switch, and she and Budgie were visiting his father in prison. He was a faceless man who sat opposite them over a cheap plastic table. Matt Budgell stood up, animated, shouting he was going to kill her father, 'and your grandfather' when he got out. Prison officers ran over and wrestled him to the floor. One turned and said to her, 'You'd better go.' As she turned, the officer handed her a bottle and said, 'Here take this.' Outside the prison Budgie took the bottle from her. Bea protested because drinking from it made her feel better. Budgie kept repeating, 'They'll smell it on your breath.'

Next morning Bea woke, troubled. There was still no response from Budgie. When she arrived at Gramps' she was thankful her dad's motor-bike was not there. She knocked the door as usual, before letting herself in. The sight she met pleased her. Gramps had a chiropodist with him. The young man with shocking pink hair had just trimmed Gramps' toe-nails and was in the process of putting the finishing touches to each foot with a nail file.

'Look here,' said Gramps, 'this is the life.'

'Hiya,' said the young man kneeling before Gramps. 'I'll bet you're Bea. I feel I know you, I've heard so much about you!'

'Gramps, what have you been saying?'

'I'm Jerry. Roy here's told me that you're going to play for England because you can't stop scoring goals.'

'Hmm, I don't know about that.'

Standing up and putting away his array of tools, Jerry said, 'Right, that's me. I need to hurry. I'll see you in about six weeks, Roy. And good luck to you, Bea. I'll see myself out.' He left them, singing as he went.

Bea said, 'He seemed nice. I suppose you've turned him into a football fan.'

'I like him coming around. I'm a bit more comfortable with a bloke seeing to me, somehow. Don't get me wrong, the girls who come in are marvellous.' Gramps tutted to himself, 'It's just me I suppose.'

Bea wondered how to approach the issue of Matt Budgell with Gramps, while she pondered, she went to the kitchen to put the kettle on. There were dishes in the sink, and a thin left-over whiff of a well-cooked meal. That'll be Dad from last night, but she was annoyed he hadn't washed the dishes. She opened the tap to pour hot water over a blob of washing-up liquid while the kettle boiled. She rinsed the corny *World's Best Grandad* mug, picked one she preferred out of the cupboard for herself, and flung tea bags in.

'You're *fantasmagoragle* you are,' said Gramps, taking his mug of tea from her.

'Can I make you something to eat? I don't want you losing any more weight,' she said.

'I'm fine, thank you, darling. One of the girls will call later with a spot of lunch and that does me until your father gets back this evening.'

Whilst they drank their tea Gramps started reminiscing again. Although he repeated stuff she'd heard before, there was usually some little bit that Bea hadn't heard that made up her family's history; stories to hand on and hand down. Bea loved to hear about her grandmother.

'Those hospital Sisters don't get the respect they used to. Now, your Gran was a Sister, never missed a shift, not one. And a Sister in those days carried authority. Their word was law. She was a proud lady, your Gran.'

'I do remember her y'know, Gramps.'

'I know. She never wanted you to see her when she was sick in a hospital bed. I don't know why, but she wouldn't have it, you nor our Tisha… Your dad had a twin y'know,' Gramps said almost whispering.

That took Bea by surprise. She had her cup halfway to her lips but it stayed there. She lowered it slowly and waited.

'A little girl,' he said. 'The thing we…the thing your Gran couldn't understand is why *she* died. She came out first, y'see. First born, she was the eldest. Complications with her birth, never affected the second baby, your dad. He was waiting, content, while his sister was struggling for her life, God love her. They said, if she'd lived, chances are she'd 'ave been damaged, brain damaged. So, there we are. Still, she'd 'ave been loved all the same.' The old man stopped and took a sip of his tea. He looked intensely sad.

'You never told me that story, Gramps, why not?'

'Why?' he asked refocussing on her. 'Well, lots of things happen in a life, darling. Some things you don't speak about. I don't think I've ever spoken about her to anyone but your Gran. Maybe it was just time for me to tell you. It came to me and so there you have it.' He looked over to his granddaughter and gave a soft smile. 'Winnifred Letitia we called her, after my mother, Winnifred.'

'And Letitia?'

'Means joy…happiness.'

Bea moved, brought up the stool and sat next to him. She placed her hand on his and saw he had that look again. Tears started to run down the old man's face. 'If things'd gone right she'd 'ave probably been the clever one, after her mother. Not a bloody fool like Brian, he took after me, forty years and a clock to show for it.'

Bea decided to stay with Gramps. She mustn't let herself cry, feeling if she did she'd be no use to him. She said, 'Can I get you anything, Gramps?'

This took a while to register, then he replied, 'Get me anything? No. No, darling you can't get me anything. You give me all I need from you by being *you*.'

After that, Bea couldn't find a right time to raise her burning issue about Matt Budgell.

In the gentle silence between the two Bea felt no need to talk. Then out of the blue, Gramps asked, 'Are you still doing our you-know-what?'

'I am, of course. And, I don't know, Gramps, but ever since the magic medal I just seem to have got better and better. I wonder about it, like, what's in it, how it works. I remember what you said, that time we agreed that strange things happen in the world, things we can't explain, and stuff... You asked me did I believe in magic. I didn't then, but now I'm not so sure.'

Gramps threw back his head and let out the heartiest laugh Bea had heard from him for a long, long time. Shortly afterwards he fell asleep. Bea lifted the old wool blanket he kept nearby and laid it over his legs. Then she kissed him on the forehead and slipped out of the house as quietly as she could.

On her way home, rather than walking straight on toward their school and over the bridge, Bea turned left to go past the station for a change. By chance, her mum emerged from the shop opposite with a carrier-bag full.

Bea waited for her to cross. 'What we got?' she asked, eyeing the bag.

'Ah, nothing for us. Stuff I promised I'd collect for old Roger.'

Bea told her mum about the afternoon spent with Gramps, the way he went on, and the story of the twin. 'Did you know Mum?'

'Yes. Your Gran told me, but so much happens in a life, unless you pick up every little thing…'

'Not exactly little though was it?'

'I was close to your Gran, as close as you could get by the time she passed away. The tragedy wasn't a secret, but she only really talked about the baby towards the end of her life. I suppose such an enormous thing as that demands to be aired when you know…or, you feel that…'

Both remained quiet and thoughtful for the rest of their journey. Sandy walked on to deliver her bagful of stuff, while Bea opened their front door and went straight upstairs to her room. Sitting on her bed, she reached under the pillow. The magic medal lay there as she'd forgotten to slip it into her pocket that morning. Rubbing the medal between her fingers, she examined it for the thousandth time. She went into a daydream, replaying Gramps running after a ball in the park, walking unsteadily to meet her in the gardens, and finally sitting in his chair laughing. She smiled, the images made her happy; And why not?

25

Bea woke the next morning with a mix of emotions. A light training session was arranged for later, followed by a team meeting with the coaches in preparation for the following day, when Lewes were set to play their Cup quarter-final knockout match. Oddly for her, Bea felt sluggish. She was still angry, at herself because she'd been slow to piece together issues regarding the attack on Gramps, and with Budgie…it made no sense for her to be angry, but she was…just because.

She couldn't eat anything for breakfast. In the kitchen she let the tap run, filled a tumbler full of water and gulped it down in one go. She poured boiling water into a mug with some instant coffee and sat down with her phone. She texted Budgie in caps: SOME FRIEND YOU TURNED OUT TO BE THANKS FOR NOTHING.

Nothing came back. It was three days since their walk, when she'd felt close to him and sympathised with what he told her about not being able to live with his family. She felt sure Budgie either knew or had his own suspicions, but perhaps had been slow, as she had been, to put the pieces together until she had actually spoken of the attack upon her grandfather.

Bea went upstairs and changed into her football kit. Despite it only being light training she decided to place the medal in her boot anyway, but didn't bother going through her match-day ritual. She put on her warm jacket and shoved a change of clothes in her kit-bag. Instead of coming home for a shower she would call with Gramps and have lunch there with him. When she arrived at the ground the others greeted her as usual, but for once her heart wasn't in it. She went through the motions in the session and no one really noticed she wasn't trying. If anyone did, they put it down to saving herself for the big match. Neither did anyone think anything when Bea remained quiet over the course of their team talk, when tactical plans were reviewed for the game. Everyone wished each other the best and said, 'See you tomorrow.'

Bea knocked at Gramps' door and let herself in. She came upon him sat in his pyjamas and was immediately alarmed. He appeared tired and ill, and older. He looked up and said, 'I feel funny.' He was frowning, and Bea could see beads of sweat on the old man's brow. 'I'm so sorry I haven't been to see you play,' he said.

Bea knelt down at his side. He kept repeating his apology. She knew this was serious.

'Stop, Gramps, shhh now,' she said, explaining what she was doing as she phoned the Emergency Services to summon an ambulance. The questions they asked seemed to go on and on. 'Can you be as quick as possible please?' she begged. 'I'm sorry, but it's my grandfather.'

Bea rushed to the kitchen to get a glass of water for him. She helped him hold it to his lips while he took a sip.

'Can you speak, Gramps?'

'I feel funny. I feel dizzy. I don't know.'

'Are you in pain?'

Gramps hesitated. 'I think I've got a headache. Have you seen Brian? Her name was Winnifred Letitia, named after our Tisha.'

Bea was concerned that Gramps was making little sense. She pulled over a stool, placed two cushions and lifted Gramps' legs. She fought desperately to be clear-headed and confident as the situation demanded of her. She wished she'd applied herself to learning First-Aid when a chance was offered to her. *Instead I was too busy playing football!* She wasn't in a position to offer anything but comfort and company to the man she loved most in the world.

Gramps squeezed Bea's hand. 'Olivia will be here in a bit. It'll be alright then.' His speech was clear in spite of his mind obviously ranging all over the place. 'He's not here,' said Gramps. 'I think he's playing football.'

That must be about Dad, she thought. 'That's right, Gramps. Yes, he would be,' she said trying to reassure him. A loud rap at the door startled Bea as she listened to the old man.

'That'll be Brian now,' he said.

Bea greeted the paramedics, a man and a woman, who went straight in past her, business-like and professional. Immediately the woman knelt beside Gramps, told him her name was Lauren, and asked if he could tell her *his* name.

'Royston Bagshot of course,' said Gramps.

'What day is it today, Roy?'

Frowning, it was obvious Gramps struggled with that question.

'Do you know who the Prime Minister is?'

No one, including Bea, could help but smile when Gramps replied, 'Yes, Lauren, he's a useless bastard.'

Once again, Bea and her Gramps shared an ambulance. Lauren stayed in the back with them and encouraged Bea to keep talking to him. She added it was a good sign that he knew about the Prime Minister. Bea smiled, holding Gramps' hand, determined to remain composed and ready to do anything she was asked.

Bea had not spoken to her father since their exchange on Sunday, but once at the hospital she phoned her dad's number. He didn't pick up. She sent a text explaining where they were. She sent the same to her mum, but knew she might not see it until the end of her shift.

The time dragged on until Brian eventually arrived. No mention was made of the previous tense exchange between them and it was almost early evening before a doctor explained the position as he saw it. He thought Gramps' condition was possibly related to the recent attack on him and the injury to his head. Brian struggled with that information, not wanting to believe that, somehow, his actions had brought the incident about.

'He may need surgery,' said the doctor.

'Brain surgery?' queried a shocked Bea.

'I'm afraid that *is* likely. We will have to wait until the consultant examines him before we can be certain. Obviously, if surgery is needed I'm unable to say when it might take place. For the moment Mr Bagshot is *comfortable*.

Bea's phone bleeped. A message from her mum. Bea rang her back, gave her an update and said that she wanted to stay the night but her mum insisted she come home. She was to telephone a taxi and never mind the expense.

'I can't take you on the bike,' said her dad. 'No helmet.' Whilst father and daughter sat waiting for the taxi to ferry Bea home, he said, 'Can you forgive me for the other day? You caught me out, Bea. I don't want there to be bad feeling between you and me.

'The man you mentioned is a bad 'un. At the beginning I thought he was a friend, but he's ruthless. He's dangerous and...I need you to forgive me...'

Bea was only half-listening as he continued on and she certainly couldn't summon the energy to talk to him at that moment. Was Dad so upset about Gramps that he was talking for the sake of it? Bea was abruptly hit by the terrible realisation that she was the grown-up here. Suddenly she was aware of acute sympathy for her hopeless father and the realisation dawned that they would never be able to function as a family unit again.

'Here's the taxi, honey,' he announced, glancing up. 'Away you go. Safe home now. I shouldn't say too much to Mum about what I said until I have a word with her.'

In the taxi Bea was silent, her head in a peculiar empty space, grateful that the driver didn't want to talk. What did he say that he thinks Mum isn't aware of? Her mind turned over, dancing from one thing to another at random. The match tomorrow, she thought, will have to go ahead without me. Once again, all the important things in her life had lost their meaning.

She drifted, back before Gramps, before the Budgell question, before Alana's day of freedom to an evening with her last week. Bea had been transfixed by the alluring, enigmatic *Kahlo* self-portrait, demanding to know more about her.

'That's why I'm so bored,' said Alana. 'I'm pissed off being so...so ordinary.' She began to tell Bea what she knew about the artist she'd recently discovered, how exceptional she was as a person in adversity, passionate, eccentric, tragic. Bea was equally taken with the image of the woman artist and the story

Alana related, amazed that she'd been hardly known until long after her untimely death, intrigued when Alana revealed Kahlo was bi-sexual. Bea wanted to learn more, and suggested they should research her together.

'That'll cure your boredom. We could do, like, a project either now or at school when you get back.'

'I wish I could paint,' said Alana. 'I want to do something extraordinary. I'm just fucking fed up.'

'We *will* find something, Lan, we love life…like, in spite of everything. Anyway, maybe you can paint. Don't painters go to art school, or art college, or something? They learn how to draw and paint.'

'I'd never be any good. The only thing I can draw is sympathy. I don't get what the hell I'll ever do with my life.'

'From what you say, Frida Kahlo probably asked herself the same questions. And look what she achieved, her face all over Alana Lane's bedroom walls. How good's that?'

Alana smiled, 'I wish I could go back and ask her how she made sense of her life. I'm waiting for my life to begin again, Bea.'

'Hey, you're on a downer. It'll pass, Yin Yang, right?'

Yin Yang thought Bea now, as the taxi pulled up outside her house. Her mum opening the door to pay the driver jerked her back to reality. Her phone bleeped as she got out of the car. It was Budgie, with a text message.

26

Bea hadn't a clue what time it was, only that the light had faded. It must be early evening. Tisha hugged her and the girls sat down on the sofa together. Bea took deep breaths and looked about her, comforted by her familiar surroundings, the trappings of home. This is where I'm safe, she thought, safe with Mum and Tisha.

'I'm going to put some sausages under the grill,' said Sandy.

'Nothing for me, Mum, I couldn't,' said Bea. She followed her mother into the kitchen to let the tap run for a glass of water but was distracted with the need to run upstairs to the bathroom to pee, or maybe she should read Budgie's text, or? Or?

In the end she went back into the living room, sat with her sister and her mum, and told them all about Gramps. Bea related events slowly, covering everything that had happened since she'd found him. When she told them what Gramps had said in reply to the question about the Prime Minister, Tisha laughed. When they both looked at her she looked down slightly shamefaced in the circumstances, although there was no need for embarrassment.

'Mum, can I give you a number to ring for me? I want you to tell them I can't play the match tomorrow.'

'It's your big quarter-final, are you certain you won't play?' asked Sandy.

'I'm sure.'

'Okay, if you're sure.'

'They need to know the quicker the better, Mum, to prepare without me.'

After Sandy had made the call for Bea the three sat contemplating, disturbed only when Sandy's phone buzzed. The call was quickly over.

'That was your Dad,' she said. 'No news, just checking that you're alright.'

After their talk was exhausted and there seemed little left for anyone to usefully add, Bea decided she would say goodnight. It was not near bedtime, but she felt she wanted to be alone. In her room, she undressed and put some sounds on down low. She took out her phone to read the text from Budgie.

B just got your texts..lots happened..call me i'm not in lewes have 2 c u 2 tell all.

Bea thought for a moment then started to text back. But everything she tried to say seemed wrong. *My grandfather is dying because of you*, was wrong. *I hate you and never want to see you again*, was wrong. *You didn't pick up when I needed you*, was wrong. *What was so important you couldn't get back to me?* was wrong. *I'm worried and upset and don't know what to do*, was right, but no text was sent, no call made. When Bea woke multiple times during the night, it surprised her because she thought she hadn't been asleep in the first place.

The following morning, with Tisha in bed and Sandy left for work, Bea headed for the bus to the hospital. She walked to the bus station with her hands deep in her puffa jacket, without a plan and unsure what she was going to do or say when she reached the Royal Sussex Hospital. It was a different Bea than the one from the day before. She could sense herself becoming emotional. She decided to phone Jack, but the bus was packed and the engine noise was overwhelming, so she decided to wait. By the time she got off the bus the rain was beating down and the world seemed a harsh and unforgiving place. When she got to the hospital she hesitated, confronted by queues of people at the reception and nurses and others in a range of uniforms walking, practically running, adding to the organised chaos. She looked around and walked over to a seat. She phoned Janis.

'Bea? Where are you? What's happened?'

'Aunt Janis, I'm at the hospital. I don't know what to do.'

'You sound upset, love. Is it your Gramps? What have you heard...who's with you?'

Bea sobbed into the phone, 'I haven't s-spoken to a-anyone yet, everything is mad here. No one is taking notice of anyone. I c-can't get near to speak to anybody.'

'Bea, stay where you are, love, I'm coming over now. I'll be with you quick as I can. Okay? Do you hear me?'

'Yes.'

Bea sat ignored and feeling helpless, desperately trying to make sense of everything. She attempted to dry her eyes but had only the backs of her hands to use. She waited, thinking, how could I be so composed one day, but so irrational the next? It was because yesterday I had to be there to ensure I got help for Gramps. She felt her jeans but there was no reassuring contour. She'd left the medal under her pillow again. She closed her eyes, took deep breaths, and gradually began to feel calmer.

She gave a start when Janis touched her shoulder, not knowing how long she'd been waiting. Janis sat beside her.

'I've spoken to Reception and your Gramps is comfortable. No visitors are being allowed until at least tomorrow. Come home with me, Bea. We can stay together for the rest of the day and I'll speak to your mum when she's finished work.' Minutes later the pair were in a taxi heading back to Lewes.

Bea was comforted when she heard Petra inside sniffing along the bottom of the front door. Petra made an extra fuss of her because she hadn't seen her for days.

'Where's Jack?'

'He's at his wheelchair basketball. Let's have a coffee,' said Janis, 'then we'll have to take Petra for a run if it stops raining. How's that sound?'

'Good,' said Bea. She hung up her coat, and followed Janis. She sat on a kitchen chair fondling Petra's ears. The dog leant her back against Bea's legs watching Janis in case she reached for the biscuit tin. Janis didn't, so Petra collapsed on her belly at Bea's feet.

'I don't know what to say to make this any easier, Bea. In the meantime all you can do, all any of us can do is to let things take their course. Okay?'

'I know,' said Bea, taking the offered mug of coffee.

'Are you playing this week?'

'No. I couldn't with what's going on.'

'Of course, it's the match this afternoon' said Janis softly. 'It's still raining. We won't go out yet a while.'

Later, Bea sat in front of the television wondering if she should phone Budgie while Janis was upstairs. But what to say to him? If it stopped raining she could take Petra out on her own, and phone then. She spent the rest of the morning dwelling on the idea of what to say to him. By lunch time Bea realised how hungry she was, and they tucked into fish pie with a side salad Janis had prepared. During the meal Bea repeated bits of how she'd found Gramps confused. Afterwards, as usual, Janis declined her offer to help with washing up.

Bea took Petra into the living room and buried her face in the dog's soft ears, with their musty smell she so perversely enjoyed. Then her phone buzzed. The screen showed, *Budgie*, but she didn't pick up. Eventually, Bea decided that unless they spoke, her mind would explode; she texted telling him to call her back in an hour.

Bea went to Janis and thanked her for what she'd done. 'I'm alright, really. I think I should go home now. I have things to do and, well...'

'Whatever you think best, love. Don't you want to wait for Jack?'

'No, we'll speak later. It's just that... The rain's easing, too, I need the walk, and—'

'Bea, it's okay. You don't have to explain. Off you go, and I'm here, okay?'

Bea left, but by the time she reached home she still didn't know what she would say to Budgie. His text had said lots had happened. What would he have to tell her? The house was empty. She went upstairs to her room and waited. The longer time went on the more nervous she became, but, she asked herself, what have I got to be nervous about? She started to do sets of push-ups, resting for two minutes in between. Then her phone buzzed. She snatched it up.

'Hello.'

'Bea?'

She said nothing, and waited, making him speak. 'I don't know how to start this,' he said. 'Please...'

'What would you like me to say?' said Bea, suddenly feeling her blood rise. 'That, if it wasn't for your father, my grandfather wouldn't be in hospital right now fighting for his life? That you should have had the guts to tell me on Saturday and not run off like you did? That you should have picked up when I wanted to speak to you on Sunday?'

'What did you say? Your grandfather is—'

'Yes, you heard right. I found him slumped yesterday in his chair and now he probably needs an operation. He might need brain surgery.'

'Bea, I don't know what to say. I'm so sorry.'

All the pent-up anger at the image of Gramps and her rage at who was responsible for beating him drained from her like a plug had been pulled from a bath. She slumped, feeling worn out. 'Are you?' she managed.

Budgie said, 'Yes. And it isn't what you think. That Sunday night, police raided my house. They arrested Jamie and took me in as well, into care. So much has happened. I had to go stay with a family. It was an emergency. I didn't have my phone, the police had it. Then last night I was moved to my uncle's, the one I told you about in Hastings and that's when the police gave me my phone back and I saw your messages.'

He's a child in care, thought Bea, even though it seemed ridiculous to think of him as a child.

'Are you calling from Hastings?'

'Yes, but my uncle has to go to Lewes on Friday on business. I can come with him. Will you meet me?'

'People don't want me to see you,' she said.

'I wish you would. There are things I need to explain properly. Bea...I'm not my father.'

That evening there was a lot of activity. Before Sandy came in from work, Bea learned from a teammate they had won and were through to the Cup semi-final to be played in three weeks' time.

After they'd finished their evening meal Janis called in with Jack, and then Brian called and the house was full. Jack was appropriately subdued knowing what this situation meant to Bea. Bea was quiet, too, starting to realise that life never stood still. Her destiny wasn't planned. She would make herself the person she wanted to be.

Brian let the family know Gramps had a date for surgery. All being well, his operation was set for next Monday.

27

On Thursday evening Bea got ready for training. She put on her kit, placed her medal in her boot and her boots in her kit-bag. She was looking forward to a good work out, but first she faced everyone to apologise for missing their crucial cup-tie. She told them what had happened on the morning of the match.

'I need you to know it was impossible for me to play and if you choose to start without me in the semi I understand.'

'What's important is that your grandfather pulls through, Bea,' said the coach. There was a chorus of, 'Yes,' and, 'That's true, Bea,' echoed among her teammates.

All the girls offered their sympathy and best wishes for his operation next week.

'If you'd been there we would've won by more than one nil.'

'Yeah, true. But we won.'

'Chin up, we love you, girl.'

Bea was humbled. She went out and trained like a girl possessed, knowing how good a robust workout made her feel. For once, however, the famous natural endorphins wouldn't work their magic. The team had another league game on

Sunday, but at the end of training Bea calculated she was too worried about Gramps and was in no mind to play.

That evening she and her mum got ready to visit him. In her bedroom she caressed the magic medal that gave her some comfort as the live link between them. On the train to Brighton she felt its contour in her jeans. She kept it in her palm during the visit but left the hospital upset. Gramps had slept throughout the hour they'd spent with him, even though they were assured he was doing as well as they could expect. He was conscious but sedated. Bea decided she wouldn't see him again until after his operation.

Overcast early on, Friday turned into a beautiful mild spring morning with thin clouds stretching in lazy swirls over a blue sky. Bea approached Cliffe Bridge and saw him looking out for her. He spotted her from a distance and when they came together they were awkward.

'Shall we walk along the river again?' Budgie suggested. Bea didn't reply, but moved along with him in that direction.

'I'm not sure I should even be here…with you,' she said after a moment.

Budgie's shoulders were bent in that familiar way. 'Bea, I'm asking you to listen to what I've got to say. After that, if you don't want to see me, I'll understand. I'll understand, and…I won't bug you. You won't even have to see me in school.'

'What d'you mean?'

'I'm in Hastings now. I can't travel all the way here every day. I'll be joining a new school there.'

'Oh. Right, I get it.'

A soft breeze picked up as they walked. When they came next to the river Budgie broke off a slim twig from a tree. Bea frowned but decided to say nothing. He slashed at small stones on the path, or at nothing in particular, and started to talk about his brother.

'That night the police raided, they took me along with Jamie. I told you, they kept my phone and then had to find me accommodation because I wasn't allowed to be in the station overnight. A couple of days later my Uncle Wilf agreed I could stay with them, so…that's me for the time being. Jamie's remanded in custody.'

'What's he done?'

'Dealing mostly, and theft.'

'Ah,' said Bea. 'And how do you think things will work out for you?'

'I don't know my uncle that well, but we seem to get on. His wife, my aunt, I'd never met her before, but she seems to like me.'

'It'll be tough for you, changing school and everything.'

'It doesn't worry me that much. I'll leave as soon as I can and hopefully start to learn a trade, maybe I'll be an electrician like my uncle.'

'Sounds okay if it works for you,' said Bea, whose mood was flat.

Budgie was anxious to come to the point. 'Can I ask about your Gramps?'

'Do you want me to repeat how much my Gramps means to me? Shall I repeat I don't know how I'd handle it if he dies?'

'You don't have to. I already know it. And I'm not expecting to hear you say anything to make me feel better.'

'Good.' After a moment, Bea asked, 'How much *did* you know exactly?'

'About?'

'You said you heard bad things being hatched in that house. What bad things? Was it anything to do with my family?'

'Bea, I wonder if you can understand. Things were very difficult for me.'

'Well, you know something? I am genuinely sorry about that. But if you knew...if you know anything, Budgie, you'd better do the right thing. Otherwise I want nothing to do with you.' Bea took deep breaths as she'd trained herself to do.

Budgie ran a hand through his long hair, then took a deep breath of his own. 'I heard lots of things that made me sick. It's a small house, but I did my best not to listen at doors for information. I could have heard more...I know what I've got to do.'

'What?'

'My father could be released in a few weeks. I need to make sure he stays where he belongs.'

That statement could mean nothing or could mean a lot. She was prepared to wait. They decided to sit on the wall running alongside part of the river. Budgie threw the twig he was carrying into the water, and they both watched it carry away, bobbing up and down on its uncertain journey.

Bea was so unsettled on the day of Gramps' op that she simply couldn't start back to school that Monday. Sandy was forced to take the day off to be with her. The two of them walked to Janis' for lunch, but even Petra couldn't succeed in cheering Bea up. Nevertheless, after lunch she said she'd walk Petra on her own, so off they set on a day of filmy cloud with a mild calm air. Bea didn't take Petra's ball. Without her playthings Petra simply followed her nose and allowed her instinct to occupy her. That suited Bea, deep in thought. The tactic she'd developed from Jack, focussing on a task, one idea or activity at a time let her down. There was only one stubborn thought that refused to dilute. Dad was at the hospital. He was the one who would deliver news of Gramps, for good or ill. In her hand Bea squeezed their magic medal until it hurt.

A shout of 'Oi!' shook her out of her trance. A man nearby was pointing behind her where Petra had left a mound of poo. 'Just to let you know,' he added. 'I'm sure you don't want to leave that there.'

Bea was annoyed, more because the man probably thought she didn't give a damn. 'Right, No, of course,' she called, and turned to scoop the poop. As she turned to look for a doggy-bin the man was walking back toward her. Bea tensed and held the bag loosely, figuring she'd launch it at him if he got weird.

'Excuse me,' he said, 'I have to ask, aren't you the girl, the footballer who plays for Lewes?'

'Uh, yes, that's right,' she said, a bit surprised this man had recognised her. He looked ordinary enough, friendly, so she relaxed.

'You're the one that scores all the goals! Thought it was you.'

Bea smiled, unaware this was practically the first time she hadn't had Gramps in her head.

'I hope you don't mind my asking, just wondering, have you heard anything from other clubs at all?'

Bea considered the circumstances. Stood with a bag of warm poop in her hand, approached by a stranger in a park, pleasant enough looking and sounding, but she wasn't prepared to get into a conversation just now. Still, it was a strange question for him to ask.

'Not really, no. Why?'

'Actually, I do a bit of scouting.'

'I'm happy playing for Lewes just now, thanks.'

'I totally understand. Well, good luck. Maybe see you again. Bye.' And with that the mystery admirer went on his way.

When they got back Bea went off to wash her hands whilst the dog followed her nose as usual, licking the hands of Janis and Sandy before plopping down at Janis' feet. Waiting for Jack to arrive home the three sat discussing the world for an hour before Sandy's phone rang. It was Brian.

'Okay, okay,' said Sandy, giving Bea a thumbs up whilst listening to him. The brief call ended. 'Gramps is out of surgery and in a recovery ward, comfortable.'

'Oh. My. God.' Bea shouted, striding back and forth from one side of the room to the other, clutching the medal in a sweaty palm. Sandy and Janis both stood up until they also began to pace the floor.

'So, what do we do now?' said Janis.

'Well, *right* now, I guess we wait,' said Sandy

'I'm going out,' announced Bea. 'I have to walk. I'm okay. I'll be back in five minutes.

Outside Bea marched rapidly, going nowhere, hoping not to meet anyone she knew. There had been a score of texts that morning, all expressing hopes that her Gramps' operation would be successful. Three people in particular had texted that Bea now replied to: Jack, Alana, and, with some hesitation, Budgie. Now, each time she thought of him the alarming image of Gramps lying battered and bloodied came to mind. Nevertheless, she thanked him for his text and added that the anxious wait was on.

Brian arrived at about 7.30 that evening. Sandy asked him had he eaten at the hospital. He hadn't, so Tisha rustled together some pasta and cheese with black pepper for him, as he delivered a full account of the doctor's report.

'The consultant spoke to me. The op was successful. He managed to remove a clot that'll gradually reduce the swelling.

Dad's stable, but in an induced coma. They have to wait and see what the next few days will bring.'

'So, that means…that means Gramps is going to be alright, doesn't it?' said Bea.

Sandy said, 'It means Gramps is very ill, Bea. We have to acknowledge that.'

'I know he's very ill. I just…' but her voice cracked and great globes of tears wouldn't let her finish.

'I took it,' said Brian, 'that if the swelling goes down, then he could be discharged home fairly soon after.'

The conversation turned on how to care for Gramps when he was discharged.

Sandy said, 'We'll make sure his professional carers start again, and—'

'I want to stay with Gramps for the first few weeks after he gets home,' said Tisha.

Bea surprised all of them when she said, 'Thanks, Tish. I'm glad. That's a great idea.'

'I suppose I'll have to be relegated to the sofa,' said Brian with a weak smile.

28

The following day Bea was reluctant to go to school but her mum won the day, and off she went, too preoccupied for lessons. She tried, but found herself counting the dramas and crises life had thrown up since her birthday. She wondered if things were this way for most people after childhood days grew more and more distant. After school, Jack, Alana and she walked home together as usual. The lighter evenings were welcome and summer was definitely in the air. Jack and Alana tried their best to encourage her and cheer her up. For her part, Bea was glad the two had recaptured their closeness, and that bit made her happy.

To help divert from her major worry, Alana said, 'Not long until the semi, Bea.'

'Another three weeks yet, that's if I'm picked. I might be sub. It's not fair to put me in the side when I didn't play in the quarter.'

'You'll be in,' said Alana.

'I won't give up. There'll be other chances. I hope Gramps will still be here by the time I turn professional. That is if I'm lucky enough. I might decide on a proper job like you, Jack.'

'Oh, I've given up the idea of being a doctor.'

'Have you?' said both girls together.

'Yeah. I'm back on the gangster idea. *Robin the Hood* operating from his throne, robbing the rich instead of the other way round for a change.' The joke had worn a bit thin. No one laughed.

Alana said, 'We've been talking about careers, me and Bea. If I can't do something out of the ordinary, like go to art college and do something outrageous, I might become a hermit and live in a cave somewhere.'

'Don't do that,' said Jack. 'I could never visit a cave. Until maybe science will find a way to knit my damaged bits back together, so I could walk again.'

'I could do something connected with animals,' said Bea. 'Not a vet, though. There's nothing wrong with that, but so many say they want to go to veterinary school, the courses would be, like, impossible to get on.'

They arrived at Jack's, where Alana was joining the cousins for tea. They knew Janis planned to be out, so they had the kitchen to themselves. She'd left a cottage pie for them and while they waited for it to heat, Jack put music on and clicked the coffee machine. Bea remained quiet over their meal, aware that she couldn't keep talking about Gramps. She knew the others sympathised, but there was a limit. When Jack and Alana decided to play a computer game in his room, Bea said, 'See you guys later,' and enjoyed what for her was a slow stroll home.

She was opposite the Dripping Pan when her phone buzzed. She stopped walking and answered, 'Hello.' It was that voice she loved to absorb, delivered by the boy she tried to but couldn't dislike.

'Hi Bea, I wanted to ask about your Grandad. How are things?'

'No more word yet. He's still not awake, so…we're just waiting.'

'Right…you don't mind me phoning…to see how things are with you?'

'That's okay. What about you?'

'Things are alright, I think. I haven't got on anyone's nerves yet. I've got two little cousins here, eleven and thirteen. They seem like good kids. They're both cool with me being around. The little one wanted to know how long I was staying, but not in a bad way.'

'And school?'

'Still waiting on that. There's a Social Worker setting up a meeting with a Head near where we are, but I'm just waiting on that. Are you playing this week?'

'There's a school match next week. I might play. I probably will. It's the last game. After that I've got a Cup semi with Lewes, but that's three weeks away. The season's wrapping up now. If we get to the final, that'll be it, sometime in May.'

'Okay.'

'Budgie, you said the other day, you knew what you had to do. What did you mean?'

After a moment, he said, 'I'm not certain. I thought if anything happened to your Gramps. Then I thought, like, it already has happened. What am I waiting for?'

'Then tell me, what is it? What is it you're waiting for? Do you know something definite?'

'It's difficult…he's…my father. I'm not sure I've got enough.'

'Enough what?'

'Information, Bea…evidence.'

They still found their phone exchanges awkward, with neither being sure of the approach each should take with the other. Instinctively both wanted to keep contact, but Bea's emotions were conflicted. Was speaking to Budgie disloyal to Gramps? Budgie was torn, too, but in a very different way to Bea. He needed no convincing that his father was a bad man, yet he also knew he did not take after him. He felt he owed his father little. It was not straightforward, but for the sake of goodness he couldn't ignore a strong sense that he owed Bea the truth.

Since their last meeting Bea and Budgie had continued to exchange texts daily, always with him making the first move. Time dragged on until, three days after his op, Gramps wakened from his sedation. She visited him several times in hospital, each time finding him livelier and more with it than the time before. The change in him was remarkable. The doctors couldn't account for his pace of recovery and warned him to take things easy. Bea was overjoyed, which helped her rediscover her own zest. Whatever drugs Gramps was on, wherever his spirit had settled, he was in top form. He could hardly sit still and his improvement was so rapid that within ten days he was discharged home. Now, Bea phoned Budgie, the first time she had initiated a call, to tell him her good news.

'Oh man, that's fantastic.'

She thought he sounded relieved.

'I've got something to tell you.'

'Go on,' Bea prompted.

'Do you know whether the police visited your Gramps in hospital?'

'What?'

'I talked to my uncle about stuff and…well, he went with me to visit the police in Lewes last week. Look, it's difficult over the phone. I need to see you to explain properly, but they let us know they intended to speak to him, to your Gramps I mean.'

'But what did you say? You said you needed evidence—'

'Stop. Hold up. I can't see you because there's no magic money tree anymore. I haven't got any money to travel from Hastings.'

'Okay, so tell me as much as you can. I need to know.'

'The best way I can put it is like this. We...that is, I, sat down and told what I knew. The things I'd heard over the years, the way he treated my mother, everything. I said I'd heard him talking with his friends about your father, not specifically about your Gramps, but how they could get your dad to play ball. I was with the police for at least a couple of hours and signed a written statement.'

'How d'you feel about all that? I mean...after all he's...well you know what I'm trying to say.'

'I'm still working through that. I'm getting to speak to someone about all sorts...the Social Worker's arranging it.'

'Oh, Budgie, I know one thing,' said Bea. 'It's time I had this out with *my* father.'

Bea rounded the corner from Jack's and crossed the road to Gramps'. When she stepped in she was happy to find him with a crossword, and his radio on.

'Hey, Gramps.' She was happier still to find the old man looking so bright. He'd lost the dressings to his head, but his thinning hair would never cover the angry scar that remained midway above his left temple.

'You look great, Gramps, how'd you do it?'

'*Rage, rage against the dying of the light*, darling, or something like that,' he said smiling.

Bea gave him a peck on the cheek, and said, 'Right, you can make the tea then!'

'You help yourself my love, I'm okay.'

'I'm joking, and I'm full of coffee anyway.' She sat across from him staring into the trophy cabinet again.

She said, 'Gramps, did you get a surprise visit before you left hospital?'

At that moment chance dictated Brian's arrival, carrying his crash helmet in one hand and a box of groceries in the other. Bea set herself firmly, determined to take advantage of the fortuitous timing. Unlike previously, she was full of confidence to put any challenge to him. Her hand went to her jeans pocket. She felt the medal, now for the reckoning.

'Hullo,' said Brian, sensing a quiet in the room.

'Hello, Dad. I was just asking Gramps had he had a surprise visit from anyone while he was in hospital.'

Brian didn't answer and made his way through to the kitchen to deposit his shopping.

'Well, Gramps?'

Gramps frowned quizzically. 'What are you wondering about, my darling?'

'She's on about the police visit, Dad. Am I right?' Brian asked returning to the room and looking sternly at Bea.

'Spot on, Dad,' she said, holding her father's stare for the first time that she could remember. She was no little girl anymore. She watched his demeanour change.

Brian sat down and while Gramps remained silent he gave Bea a rundown of his acquaintance with Matt Budgell.

'No excuses,' he said, 'I was a fool...I *am* a fool.'

Bea sensed her opportunity to clarify things for herself once and for all.

'What did the police tell you? You were there when they interviewed Gramps?'

'Yes.'

'Why do you need to know all this, darling?' Gramps interjected.

She turned to face the old man. 'Because, Gramps, it was my friend who spoke to the police, and, if he is allowed, he's willing to give evidence at any trial against Budgell.'

'Your friend?' queried Gramps. 'What do you mean, Bea?'

'My friend, Steve. He's Matt Budgell's son.'

29

Mountfield School won their last match of the season in a comfortable 4-0 demolition of the opposition. Getgo stopped Bea as the teams left the pitch.

'Is something wrong, Bea?' he asked with a frown.

Bea looked at him, concerned. 'Er, no, I hope not. I don't think so. Why?'

'You only scored one,' he said, his frown breaking into a smile.

'That's not fair, Mr Marks,' she said, smiling back. 'You shouldn't do that.'

'Now for the big semi-final, eh? You must be saving your goals up for that.'

'If selected,' Bea reminded him. 'Mia stood in for me in the quarters and she got the winner. She should get my place, it's only right.'

'You're serious.'

'I am, yes,' said Bea as they approached the changing rooms. 'I'd be embarrassed to be selected before her.'

'That's not the way it works, Bea,' he said, with a sober expression that suggested fairness was elusive.

Bea thought to herself, he's probably right. I'm going to have to say something to Mia when the time comes.

Following a light training session in the week of the game to come, the time came for the team's tactical discussion. By then Mia had been told privately she would be named as one of the subs. She approached Bea and took her to one side before the girls sat down to discuss the match.

'Mia,' Bea began, but Mia cut her off.

'I just wanted to say, Bea, I know you're in, and to wish you the best of luck.' She gave her a hug.

'Mia,' sighed Bea, 'I don't know what to say.'

'There's nothing to say. If I was the coach, I'd pick you, too,' she laughed. 'The way you play only makes me want to get better and nothing would please me more than to dump you on the bench next season!' She reached out again, smiling, and the girls embraced.

The two sat together, all ears and imagination, as the team and coaching staff went over the plan to win the semi-final on Saturday.

Later the same evening at Gramps' Bea recounted the story.

'That's how it goes. She made it easy for you, credit to her. And, as she said, she'd be happy if it was her and not you in that position.' He paused. 'Do you want to tell me more about this boy, Steve?'

Bea was embarrassed by her confusion, asked to talk to the main person in her life about her friend, the son of the man who had attacked and seriously injured him. Bea sat as if looking into the distance.

'I…I'm not sure what to say, Gramps. In one way he's just someone I met in school. Bit by bit I discovered who he was…I mean, who his father is. He, Steve, he's not like them…he hates them in a way. You know his father is in prison?'

Her Gramps nodded.

'With what Steve has told the police, it could mean when his father's sentence is up, he might be remanded back into custody. He'll stay in prison if he's charged. The police weren't sure if Steve would be able to testify against his own father. They said they'd be speaking to their legal people, but they were building a case, and his statement helped.'

'I remember you telling me that people should choose their friends wisely,' said Gramps quietly. 'Makes me think of you and your dad, you're not a bit like him.'

Then Gramps switched completely. 'D'you know what? I'd like to come and watch you on Saturday.'

Bea laughed, 'No Gramps, it's too soon. You've been told to take it easy.'

'Easy–sneezy,' he scoffed.

'It's been a long while since you watched me. I'd probably get nervous now. Back then I was only a kid.'

Gramps winked at her. 'You don't need to be nervous. You've got your magic medal. I'm going to be there with you. I am.'

The following evening Brian called to say Gramps was more excited than any of them.

'If Gramps is definitely coming I want to travel with him to the match,' said Bea.

'If you do, I could hire some sort of people-carrier for the day,' Brian said. 'Let's see, so besides you, and me driving, we've got Gramps, Mum and Tisha, then there's Janis and Jack. We'll need the space for his chair—'

'And a chair for Gramps and there's Alana as well,' said Bea, 'Don't forget her.'

'Okay, I'll wangle something. Leave it to me.'

Sandy was smiling listening to this. Then an awful thought crept in… When Saturday came would Brian materialise with a suitable vehicle, or would he let them down yet again? She dismissed her thought. There was just no way… He'd be lost to the family forever.

Saturday morning Alana was sitting with the Bagshots in their living room. Everyone was talking over one another when right on the appointed time, Brian pulled up in a sleek maroon people-carrier. He parked directly outside the window. Despite only briefly glancing at the vehicle, Bea immediately noticed the absentee. Jack waved from his seat in the back, whilst Brian and Janis got out. Bea went to the door leaving the others prattling with excitement. She met her dad's unsmiling face outside the front door. Looking her father in the eye, she asked, 'Where is he?'

'Okay, it's like this,' said Brian. 'Gramps isn't here, Bea. This is *your* day and he sends his best, but he's just not feeling himself. He's absolutely cursing that he—'

'Dad, I said where is he?'

'The thing is, Bea, he's gonna be just fine. I had to call an ambulance for him this morning. When he woke up to get himself ready he said he felt *funny* again, and a bit tired. I called the ambulance just to be on the safe side, but he insisted you play.'

Bea felt her insides turn over from her chest to her knees. 'I can't,' she said quietly. She turned and went inside where the rest immediately saw the expression on her face.

Sandy went quickly to the window and looked. She turned, 'Gramps?'

Brian and Janis joined them and suddenly the room was full...and quiet.

Brian repeated what he'd said to Bea outside.

Sandy took charge. 'Bea, we should do as we planned. If you go to the hospital I guarantee you will spend the whole day sitting around waiting for hours to be told Gramps is comfortable. Gramps will be upset if you don't play today, and even more upset at the thought that you didn't play because of him. Then there's your team to think of, too. You know well enough by now that if you go to the hospital you'll be wasting your time sitting about being useless, you'll be upset, your Gramps will be upset and your team will feel let down. I'm sorry, but that's how it is.'

Nobody else spoke. Sandy had said everything that was needed.

Bea let the thoughts and emotions run through her mind, over and again. She thought of Gramps and she heard his voice urging her on. Almost unconsciously, she began to nod her head. *Playing is what Gramps would want, and you know that*, she told herself.

'So, are we good?' her mum asked.

'Yes,' Bea said.

'Now, have you got everything ready?' asked Sandy.

'My bag,' said Bea, softly as if in a daze.

'Tish, go upstairs and fetch her kit-bag. Come on everybody. Jack's by himself waiting out there. Let's get going.'

Bea, lost in thought, went out with the others who were quietly chattering over seating arrangements. Jack was perched on his throne at the rear, Bea and Alana sat together just in front of him. Brian, Sandy and Janis did their best to keep a conversation going in an otherwise subdued drive to the Performance Centre at Lancing that was hosting both semi-finals.

'The only way to make any sense of the rest of today is to do it for your Gramps,' whispered Jack in her ear. Bea pressed her fingers to her temples, her thoughts racing. Tisha and Alana repeated Sandy's wise words and by the time they arrived she'd got the message. She was *playing for Gramps, so she had to go for it!*

Her teammates had arrived minutes before her and welcomed her with shouting and chatter. Bea greeted everyone back, doing her best to keep her anxiety to herself. The match was massive for the club and for all of them. The team didn't need to know. When the rush of 'hellos' and high-fives had died down, she looked around the dressing room, amused, in spite of everything, by the various ritual antics being taken up by her teammates. It hit her suddenly and with such force that her amusement turned to horror – her own ritual, their magic medal, was still lying under her pillow. But before she could think any further, the coach hustled the girls out for a series of warming and stretching exercises, before gathering them together, wishing them all good luck and ending by telling them, 'to go out and own the pitch!'

From the kick-off it was clear, by the elementary mistakes many players on both sides made, that the most prevalent thing on the pitch was nerves. Five minutes in and Bea had barely had a touch; her team were struggling to string two passes together. She managed to collect and distribute a few good backwards and sideways balls, but the opposition defenders were pressing a high line and working hard.

The half went on, tightly fought, few clear chances, a stalemate. She was soaked with sweat, but for no reward. Not one shot on target by either team. The half came to an end and she trudged off. As she sipped her water, she felt a hand on her shoulder. Brian had come to offer a few words of football wisdom. Bea hardly heard him. Her thoughts were elsewhere, on what could have been, what should be.

Taking the field for the second-half, Bea determined that even without the magic in her boot she was playing for Gramps, but still there was a block in her head. Still it was difficult to find a rhythm to her game. She began to rely on shielding the ball when it fell to her, holding it up to allow the speedy girls each side of her to run into space. It was stuff she'd learned in training with the older girls at Lewes, but it made no real impact. The game drew on. A corner or two for each side, all hacked away by defenders. A free-kick, blazed over at one end, a second blazed wide at the other. The sides were evenly matched and not one open chance fell the way of either. The players were labouring to create openings. Substitutes were thrown on. Nothing changed.

Bea half expected to be replaced, but she stayed on and determined that all she could do was ensure at the end of the game, she'd *left everything on the pitch*. She ran and ran and continually looked to take up good positions, but it was increasingly clear to her, and she felt it from the crowd too, the opposition were gaining a dominant edge. With the ball being played square across the Lewes back four, Bea sensed eyes on her. So strong was the feeling she glanced to the touchline where her family stood, but no, all were following the game.

Bea felt the hairs on her neck stand up and a tremor ran through her. She checked again. Again, no one was staring at her.

She refocussed on the match and like her teammates, began to anticipate the final whistle. The ref looked at her watch. Bea jogged toward the opposition goal while watching the Lewes' left full-back making her way down the wing. The weak cross found no one but the goalkeeper. Bea thought, *we'll be going to extra time.*

Still facing the opposition goal, she started jogging backwards towards the halfway line. The ball was thrown out to the opposition right-back, who advanced forward. Bea saw the glance, the look towards the centre-back. Bea stopped jogging backwards and accelerated forwards, anticipating the cross field ball. Sure enough, the opposition right-back squared it, the centre-back, exhausted from her efforts, watched and waited for the ball to arrive, but Bea was there, in the way. She jumped, took the ball on her chest, landed, waited for the ball to drop and then, on instinct, drew back her right foot to lash the ball on the half-volley. Her thirty-yard low drive was almost a daisy cutter, but it travelled straight as an arrow and with a mixture of luck and her precise execution, smashed into the corner of the net. The eruption of joy was deafening from the stands and from her teammates. The girls swamped Bea until the referee had to physically pull them off her. Such was the elation that when the referee actually found Bea beneath the melee she had to ask if she was okay. In her triumph the two critical missing ingredients on the day made Bea cry and laugh at the same time. The final two minutes of the game dragged by and Lewes Under16s threw the last of their energy into defending for their lives, but finally, the whistle sounded and a May Cup Final beckoned.

The victory brought a curious mix of experiences. First the jubilant emotion of the dressing room for Bea and her mates, followed by the journey home.

Jack's thoughts, like his gaze, was on Alana and his desire for her.

Alana's on Jack and what it would take for them to become a couple.

Janis and Tisha chatted, not about football, but fashion. Tisha, for once, enjoying the importance of being asked the merits of different creams, potions and lotions.

Sandy was thinking about Gramps, although her thoughts strayed to Brian and a time when he'd had the world at his feet, worshipped for his footballing ability. If only his physical strength had translated into strength of character.

And Bea, still wrapped in the glow of scoring a winning goal, concentrated her thoughts on Gramps and what was next for him.

30

Bea phoned Budgie that evening and gave him her news. 'Is life ever gonna make sense?'

'I wish I could answer that,' he said. 'Is your Gramps…is he very ill?'

'I honestly don't know. I'm being told the usual, he's *comfortable*. He was doing too much. I hadn't seen him so lively in years. And he so wanted to watch me, he was so looking forward to going to the match.'

He'd been in hospital for several days before Bea got a chance to visit him alone. *We belong to each other*, she felt it as the strongest bond she had and she knew he felt the same. She sat down next to his bed, watching and waiting. She breathed deeply and rhythmically, remaining composed and thought, if he doesn't wake I'll leave when my time is up. In a short time, his eyes flickered and he sensed her. His head didn't turn and he spoke in a whisper, 'Hello darling.'

She took his hand and caressed it with her thumb, 'Hey Gramps.'

'I know you scored. Well done.'

She hesitated for a bit, but decided to tell him. 'I forgot our *magic medal*, Gramps.'

He gave a weak chuckle, which set off a brief bout of coughing. 'Stand up so I can see you properly,' he said. Bea stood over him and each held the other's gaze.

'Now, I'll tell you,' he whispered. 'It's true I was drawn by something to that medal. I don't know what, or why, but it was a sad sight lying in with a load of junk. A medal meant for some long ago footballer that was never won. And, I couldn't make out why the metal had worn so thin. It must have belonged to someone. Someone must have owned it and held it lots and worked it a lot. Maybe kept it as some lucky charm or something. People are funny.

'You know already, we footballers are a superstitious lot. I mean, look at you. You cared about it. It meant something. It meant something when you started banging all those goals in. Sometimes we need a little help, a little faith in something. But, really, it's all down to us…to *you*.'

'I'm not going to stop believing in our magic medal now, Gramps…I'll always cherish it.'

'Here's what I need you to do. Are you listening?'

She bent lower to catch his whisper. 'Yes, I'm listening.'

'I want you to give the medal to your dad.'

'But—'

'No. It's alright. It's still our secret. You don't need it anymore. But he does, and I want you to give him the medal as soon as possible, today.'

'It's here. It's in my pocket, Gramps. I've been carrying it with me. It doesn't live under my pillow. It's—'

'He's expecting it. Please, it's very important to me, darling.'

'Of course, Gramps, if that's what you really want.'

'Good, good…you'll see he gets it, won't you? Today.'

Bea agreed, but on her journey home she'd never felt more miserable in her life.

Some days later Bea and Tisha sat together with their own thoughts on the front upstairs seat of a double-decker out of Lewes. They looked down from the bus as it gobbled noisily up the road. Their individual minds wandered.

Tisha's thoughts covered the special hurt her sister must be feeling, knowing she had always been the centre of a special relationship. Then her thoughts switched, picturing Gramps lying in the hospital bed, then back again.

Bea's hurt and disappointment lay on her like a dead weight, although she tried to focus her mind on possibilities for Gramps, what support would he need, would he ever get back to the way he was, was it that beating he took that had brought all this on? *Why did Gramps make me give our medal to Dad?*

Outside the sun was shining though the girls hardly noticed. By the time they reached their stop both of them realised that not one word had passed between them over the whole journey, though they weren't uncomfortable about it. Moreover, an unspoken acknowledgement ascended within them, a silent awareness that affection had replaced sibling irritation and love had overtaken their day-to-day family complacency. In the future it would be a good feeling. When they reached the entrance to Gramps' ward a nurse at the desk stopped them. 'Excuse me,' she said. 'May I ask who you're visiting?'

Tisha answered, 'Mr Bagshot.' Her answer struck Bea as peculiar for a brief moment. *Why is she calling Gramps, Mr Bagshot?* The nurse said she hoped they wouldn't mind, she wanted them to visit separately.

'You mean one of us at a time?' As soon as she said it, Tisha felt stupid.

The nurse smiled wanly, 'That's right.'

The sisters looked at each other and something dawned on Tisha. 'You go first, Bea.'

Without a word, Bea went through the double doors. Unlike the previous occasions she noticed the mixed smell of urine and pine. She passed beds mostly housing very elderly men, one or two flicking listlessly through papers or magazines, one or two listening to something through plugs in their ears, others lying alone with their thoughts. Only two nurses were on the ward, both busying from bed to bed and out and in to the sluice room. Bea noticed that when they moved they ran, they didn't walk, and she wondered was that a rule?

Once again Gramps was asleep. She stood over the old man who didn't sense her this time. His eyes remained shut. She pulled a plastic chair nearer the bed and sat, wondering why the image of his long-service clock had entered her head. She thought of the pride he took in telling her about his parents, and Windrush Day, his wife, her grandmother the hospital Sister, when hospital Sisters had a status and commanded respect, and she felt her strength drain from her. Bea took a tissue from the battered locker beside his bed and dabbed her eyes, begging herself not to weep. There was a tube in Gramps' hand leading from a bruise to a bottle of something on a tripod.

Then he sensed her. It had just taken him a bit of time. Gramps spoke in a hoarse whisper, 'The top drawer.'

'Something in the drawer, Gramps, you want me to open it?'

No answer from Gramps, but Bea opened the drawer. She reached in and took out a solid shiny grey cardboard box, about six inches by four inches. It had gold lettering on it, just a company name and contact details. She removed the top, and flicked back some tissue paper to reveal a shield of pale polished wood. There were words in gold lettering:

Presented to Bea on the Ball from Gramps with All My Love.

Underneath, by itself, the word, *BELIEVE*. Atop all this, dead centre, sat the magic medal buffed and shiny, flush with the surface of the shield. She begged herself again not to weep, but she couldn't speak. Instead, she held Gramps' fingers. He held hers back, and that was enough.

And that was all.

31

Gramps was cremated. Funerals are difficult, and feelings often indescribable. It pleased Bea to see quite a few of his old workmates attended, people she had no idea he was still in touch with. Why would she? There were several of the family on his side still left, and a few more from her Gran's, and people all did their best to play the parts funerals demand. There was a gathering afterwards held in Gramps' flat, where Brian had taken over the tenancy. Bit by bit it got too crowded, and Janis suggested they go across the road to hers where there was a little more room. When they left the home, where she'd spent so many hours exchanging stories with Gramps, Bea knew she would never again set foot inside there.

Every now and then Tisha and Bea had a few secret swigs of vodka, which helped, whilst older people tried to explain to her that grief was a *process*. They meant well, but a theory only partially understood, and explained in fits and starts, sounded half-baked to her. Over the days to come Bea looked up the theory, and thought it did actually make sense when she researched it properly.

Early on the morning of the funeral Budgie texted, Thinking of you, which, knowing how difficult all the circumstances were for him, too, Bea appreciated in a big way. Later on, during one of her secret tipples with Tish, she texted back, **Thanks speak soon.**

It was time for Bea to make a major adjustment in her young life. She had already made a big decision, one that took long hours of deliberation.

Once she would have told Jack and Alana, but she kept it secret from everyone, except Budgie. She phoned and told him what she'd planned.

'It was solid in the middle. I did have a go at sticking a small screwdriver in to see if I could loosen it away, but I was, like, scared to damage it. I took it into the shop where dad had had it mounted and explained to the man. He said to leave it with him.'

Budgie said, 'I think that's a great idea.'

'I'm collecting it tomorrow.'

'Do you think we'll meet up again?' he asked.

'We will. I think I could probably come to Hastings now I've got some money Gramps left me,' said Bea. 'He would have liked you...I told him about you.'

'You told him about me?'

'Yeah, not much, but he asked about you, so I told him.'

'What did you say? What did he say?'

'He more or less said that people are individuals and shouldn't have to carry burdens that belong on their parents. He put it in the context of me and my dad as an example.'

'That does sort of make me feel better.'

'I could maybe catch the train to Hastings if you wanted?'

'That'd be cool, but not this weekend. I promised I'd help my uncle and I'm on my best behaviour because I was in trouble at school.'

'What?'

234

'I told the guys at school to call me Steve but one insisted I had to be Budgie. Nobody knows me, but I guess Budgell just naturally gets Budgie. I had to put him right. I'm Steve now.'

Bea couldn't help laughing. 'I hope things are going to be okay. Nice one, Steve.'

The following day Bea called at the shop. The bell above the door issued its ding, and a man in a black and red striped Lewes football shirt looked up from his bench. 'Ah, yes,' he said, 'it's yourself!' and disappeared into the rear of the shop. In a second he came back with Gramps' shield and stood it on the counter. 'What do you think?'

Bea took it. 'Thank you so much,' she said.

'It looks good on the shield. He had a super smile didn't he? And, of course, here's the old medal.'

Bea took the magic medal gratefully, placed it safely in her pocket and made sure by patting her jeans so as to feel the thin contour. She held the shield up and looked at it again, swallowed hard, took a deep breath and just managed to expel the words, 'What do I owe you?'

'Nothing,' he smiled. 'Nothing at all.'

Brian had given Bea the trophy cabinet she'd coveted since she was a child. He needn't have, because they were all his medals after all. It sat perfectly in the corner of her bedroom opposite her bed next to the window. If she was turned that way it was the first thing she saw when she woke up. On top of the cabinet by itself sat the shield, with a photo of a smiling Gramps embedded in it. She knew he would approve, because he was still a vital part of match day for her, and always would be. The day of the Cup Final, Bea slipped the magic medal into her boot, kissed the boot, and said, 'Believe'.

Janis, Jack and Alana, Sandy and Tisha, were travelling together again, with Brian driving. Bea left home to meet the team coach outside the Dripping Pan, giving her five minutes alone with her thoughts. As she made her way over the bridge she was confident she could make sense of her life in an uncertain world.

I might not make it to the top, she thought, but I won't let anyone ever be able to say I didn't try. On an impulse she reached into her kit-bag, caressed the contour of the medal in her boot, and looked up to the sky.

'C'mon old man, we've got a match to win.'

THE END

Acknowledgements

As always with the production of a book, there are a number of people who I owe thanks to.

A big, big shout to my editor, Ian Hooper, without whom Bea would not have kicked a ball.

To Siobhan Curham for her kindness on my writing journey and initial advice when Bea was in embryo.

To my friends Guy Earl and Duncan Thompson for their encouragement.

Much appreciation to Coleg Harlech, a hand dealt by fate without which I can't think where I'd be.

An especially fond mention to Neil Evans, my history tutor, the first person to take any interest in my education, and finally to Lewes FC, for their courage and determination to bring about an actual 'level playing field'.

About the Author

Paul Sheppard is Welsh-born but spent most of his professional life in Northern Ireland where he worked as a Probation Officer. He is still a registered Social Worker, and now lives in East Sussex.

He co-edits the match-day programme for his local community-owned football club, Lewes FC.

In July 2017 Lewes announced its Equality FC campaign, becoming the first professional or semi-professional club in the world to pay their women's teams the same as its men's, to raise awareness of gender inequality in football.

This inspired the idea for *Bea on the Ball*.

Paul's had some success with published short stories, but this is his first novel. He is currently working on literary fiction for the adult market.